THE DREAM

"We're going to enter an end-of-summer horse show," Penny said eagerly. "Bones and I are going to win the blue ribbon!"

"Are you?" Mr. Billings said, his eyes twinkling. "Really think you can do it?"

"I'm going to try," Penny said with determination. "You see, my parents want me to stop coming over here—except on weekends. They don't understand. They're worried about schoolwork, but I always make the honor roll. They don't realize that it's *important* to me to ride and have a horse. Of course, it's expensive to take regular lessons, and they don't have a lot of money. That's why it's so important for me to work with Bones. I want to do something with horses for the rest of my life!" Penny stared at him with defiant eyes. She waited for him to tell her, like most grown-ups did, that it was only a dream.

Mr. Billings didn't. He laughed and patted her on the shoulder. "Well, let's get out there and show them. Don't know when I've seen such spirit!"

Other Bantam Skylark Books you will enjoy
Ask your bookseller for the books you have missed

A HORSE
OF
HER OWN

Joanna Campbell

A BANTAM SKYLARK BOOK®
TORONTO • NEW YORK • LONDON • SYDNEY • AUCKLAND

RL 5, 008–012

A HORSE OF HER OWN
A Bantam Book / February 1988

ISBN 0-553-15564-4

Published simultaneously in the United States and Canada

Bantam Books are published by Bantam Books, a division of Bantam
Doubleday Dell Publishing Group, Inc. Its trademark, consisting of the
words "Bantam Books" and the portrayal of a rooster, is Registered in U.S.
Patent and Trademark Office and in other countries. Marca Registrada.
Bantam Books, Inc., 666 Fifth Avenue, New York, New York 10103.

PRINTED IN THE UNITED STATES OF AMERICA

S   0 9 8 7 6 5 4 3 2

For my mother, with love

One

"Penny, for the last time, no!" Jane Rodgers looked up at her daughter from the checkbook she was balancing. "You cannot have a horse or riding lessons."

"*Please*, Mom! I'd pay for it out of my allowance and baby-sitting money."

"You don't make nearly enough to cover the expense of either. We're not trying to be mean, Penny, but your father and I just can't afford it."

"Mom, I'd work extra hard, get more baby-sitting jobs."

"You should start saving that money for college. This horse craziness is probably just a phase. You'll grow out of it. Before you know it, you'll lose interest in horses altogether."

"No, I won't."

"Oh, Penny, I've had a very bad day. I've just found out that Jimmy needs braces this year. Riding lessons are twenty dollars an hour, plus clothes and boots. We honestly can't afford that expense right now."

Penny sighed in disappointment and left the house for a walk. She'd never be able to persuade her parents. They had no interest in horses and couldn't understand why riding was so important to Penny. Her mother played tennis once in a while,

1

but gardening was her favorite hobby. Her father always seemed to be working. Whenever he had any spare time, he went fishing.

Penny kicked at a stray pebble on the tree-shaded roadside and headed toward her favorite spot—Mr. Billings's place. Mr. Billings was special because he owned the only horse in the suburban part of Connecticut where Penny lived. Most of the other land in the neighborhood had been split up into small lots before Penny had been born, but Mr. Billings had one of the last old farms. He didn't work it anymore except for keeping a vegetable garden and the horse.

She leaned her arms on the split-rail fence bordering Mr. Billings's pasture. Penny sighed again and pushed her long brown hair off her freckled cheek. In all of her thirteen years, she'd never wanted anything so much as she wanted to ride. If only her parents could understand how much she loved horses!

Penny gazed longingly at the horse at the far side of the field. His head was down as he grazed, and he paid no attention to her. The horse certainly wasn't much to look at. His bay coat was shaggy; his mane and tail were tangled with burrs. He was bony, although he obviously wasn't starving with all the grass in the pasture. Penny thought the horse simply needed some tender loving care.

Penny had spent countless hours standing at the fence and daydreaming. In her daydreams she performed miracles with the old horse. She groomed him until his coat shone. She fed him grain to fatten him up. She rode him and taught him to jump, to the amazement of everyone who saw what she had accomplished.

Suddenly she stood up straighter. Well, why not? Why couldn't she do all those things she dreamed about? Mr. Billings didn't seem to care about the horse. If she asked him nicely, maybe he'd let her come and help with the horse in exchange for riding. It wouldn't cost him anything.

Of course, she didn't know Mr. Billings. She'd seen him working in his garden a few times, but they'd never spoken to each other. Some of the kids in the neighborhood said he was a mean old grouch. Maybe he'd yell at her and tell her to mind her own business. Then again, she'd never know unless she asked.

Squaring her shoulders, she started along the fence toward Mr. Billings's weed-choked drive before she lost her nerve. The sight of his house and yard was not encouraging. The white two-story farmhouse needed paint, and one shutter was hanging crookedly. The shades were drawn in three of the four front windows. The grass needed to be cut, and the bushes around the house were overgrown. In fact, the only thing Penny saw that wasn't neglected was the vegetable garden behind the house.

Maybe she was crazy to risk asking Mr. Billings. But she was already climbing the front porch steps. She took a deep breath and knocked firmly on the front door. She paced nervously while she waited. No answer. Penny was losing courage, but she knocked again. This time she heard a shuffling sound within. A moment later, the door was pulled open. A white-haired man in a stained work shirt and pants peered out at her.

Before she had a chance to open her mouth, he shouted, "Don't want any. I've already got those cookies, and all the magazines I can read."

"Wait, Mr. Billings," Penny cried as he started to close the door. "That's not why I came. I came about your horse."

"My horse?"

"Yes, that's right. I'm Penny Rodgers. I live about a mile down the street. You see, I love horses," she rushed on frantically, "and I wondered if you'd let me take care of yours."

The old man paused. His bushy brows drooped over his eyes. "Why should you want to take care of my old nag? Besides, I can't afford to pay someone to look after him. He does fine on his own."

"My parents won't let me have a horse, and I want one so badly—at least a chance to ride and take care of one. You don't seem to use your horse for anything, and I'd do it for nothing."

"For nothing, eh? Well, I don't have any use for him. Thought of getting rid of him a couple of times, but he's no youngster. Didn't think anyone would want him. I bought him years back to do some farm work and pull a cart for my grandchildren. They moved away, and I don't farm any more." He studied her with squinting blue eyes. "You want to ride?"

"Yes . . . and I'd do everything that needs to be done for the horse if you'd let me."

4

"He's never been ridden. He's only broken to harness."

"I could train him."

"Persistent, aren't you?" But the old man's mouth turned in a slight smile. "Know what you're doing? You had experience with horses?"

"Some." That wasn't a lie, if you could count what Penny had learned from books, a few free lessons, and going to the stables to watch her friend, Jan Gilman, ride.

Mr. Billings seemed to relent. "Suppose it wouldn't hurt. The old boy could use some attention. I don't have time or energy for him now. I'll have to think about the riding, though. I don't want any lawsuits."

"For a start, could I groom him and start exercising him a little?"

"Hmmm," he said, considering. "Well, come and have a look. Once you get a good look at him, you may change your mind."

He stepped out onto the porch, and with Penny following, went down the steps and across the shaggy lawn. The side pasture fence ran alongside his drive. He paused at the fence and gave a sharp whistle.

The horse immediately lifted his head. His ears perked, and he trotted toward the fence.

"His name's Bones, by the way," the old man said and chuckled. "Fits him, don't you think?"

Penny silently agreed. The horse did seem to have an awful lot of bones protruding from his body, but Penny realized it had more to do with his rangy build than lack of food. He stood about sixteen hands, a fairly tall horse, but Penny was five feet six and still growing.

Bones stuck his head over the fence and nudged Mr. Billings. The horse obviously felt affection for his owner.

Mr. Billings rubbed a hand over Bones's neck. "Sorry, old boy, I don't have any carrots on me."

Penny patted the other side of the horse's neck and scratched behind his ears. The horse had usually ignored her before when she'd come to the fence. "How old is he?"

"Mmmm." The old man fingered his chin. "About twelve, thirteen . . . I've lost track."

"Then he's not so old. Horses sometimes live till thirty."

"He's not a youngster either, and he's set in his ways. He hasn't had much to do these past years, except eat."

"What do you feed him?"

Mr. Billings chuckled again. "You're looking at it. Plenty of grass in that pasture. In the winter, I buy hay. Got a stall for him in the barn." He motioned to the weathered brown building behind the pasture. The barn certainly needed a good coat of paint, but it looked sound and watertight.

"You don't give him any grain?" Penny asked. Although Penny had no practical experience, she'd read every book on horse care that she could get her hands on.

"Why give him expensive grain? It's not like he's doing anything to burn it off. He'd be scampering around here like a colt with a few oats in him."

That piece of information pleased Penny. She looked the horse over again. He was definitely scruffy. He was still shedding his winter coat and was ragged and mud-caked from rolling in the pasture. He certainly didn't look like a Thoroughbred, but Penny was sure she saw some decent lines underneath. Immediately her imagination went to work. She envisioned his coat gleaming, his mane combed free of tangles, some weight on his bones. "What kind of horse is he? Do you know his breeding?"

"Breeding? None that I know of. I bought him from a farmer upstate when he was a two-year-old. Didn't cost me much, if that tells you anything. Probably got a touch of draft horse in him . . . maybe some Morgan."

"He doesn't look like a workhorse."

"Big bones. You still want to do it?" The old man's question interrupted her thoughts.

"Yes!" Her light brown eyes were wide with excitement as she looked up at him. "You'll let me?"

"If you want to waste your time."

"Oh, thank you, Mr. Billings! Can I come tomorrow? I'll need to get some brushes first—"

"I got some old stuff hanging around here. Let's take a look in the barn."

Bones followed them along the rail as they walked down the drive and into the barn. Mr. Billings showed her the big box stall that was Bones's winter stable, then went into a neighboring stall that was cluttered with boxes, barrels, and old tools— not to mention cobwebs galore. Penny sneezed.

7

"Dusty in here, isn't it." He went to the far wall and opened a rough wooden chest. "What have we got in here?" He dug around and extracted several brushes, a currycomb, and a halter that Penny knew would clean up with some saddle soap. "Forgot I had half this stuff," he said as he handed his finds to Penny. "Use what you can." He rose and pressed his hands to the small of his back. "Getting old. Barn's never locked, so come by when you want. Like I said, all he's done these past years is eat. I wouldn't get my hopes up. You can't make a silk purse out of a sow's ear."

"I know that, Mr. Billings," Penny said respectfully. But silently she added to herself, "But I'm sure going to try!"

When the old man went back to the house, Penny spent a few minutes making friends with the horse. Bones didn't object to the attention and conversation, but when he realized she didn't have any treats for him, he simply turned and walked away, ignoring her calls. Mr. Billings was right— Bones *was* set in his ways. But she'd change that!

In her excitement, she nearly skipped all the way home. Should she tell her parents what she was doing yet? Maybe she'd wait a few days, and then mention her new project casually. If they realized she was trying to help out Mr. Billings, maybe they wouldn't object.

That night she pored through her horse books, making a list of what she would need: hoof pick, sponges, a bag of grain, a saddle and bridle. But where was she going to find a saddle she could afford? She'd saved over a hundred dollars from

8

her allowance and baby-sitting money, but a good saddle would cost more than that. She'd need to think about it—but she had plenty of time before she tried to ride Bones.

There was a knock on her bedroom door. "Penny?"

"Yes, Mom."

Her mother pushed the door open. Her eyes went to the books strewn all over the bed. "Are you reading those horse books again? What about your homework?"

"It's done."

Her mother shook her head and sighed. "I wish you could find something else to interest you. Something more . . . practical and useful. How about some music lessons? They aren't as expensive, and we've got the piano—"

Penny wrinkled her nose.

"Well, the dishwasher's done. Come out and empty it, please."

"Okay. I'll be right there." Penny reluctantly began to gather her books together.

Penny couldn't wait to get to school the next morning and talk to her best friend, Jan. She would be as thrilled as Penny about Bones because Jan had been taking riding lessons since she was six.

"You'll never guess what's happened," Penny exclaimed when they met outside their homeroom.

"Your parents said you can take lessons."

"No, but it's almost as good. I've found a horse to take care of and ride!"

9

"You have! Where? What horse?" Jan's blue eyes were sparkling, and her dark blond ponytail bobbed in her excitement.

"Mr. Billings's. Remember I told you about the horse up the road at the old farm?" With the words tumbling out of her mouth, Penny told Jan of the previous afternoon's adventure.

"Amazing! When are you going over? Can I come?"

"Of course! Take the bus home with me this afternoon—or do you have lessons?"

"No, and I'll get my mom to pick me up after. Oh, Penny, now we can go riding together!"

"I know! But I've got a lot of work to do. He's never been ridden."

"I'll help you. I know lots about training—"

"Oh, yes, I just *love* horses," a shrill voice piped up beside them.

The girls turned around. "Oh, go away, Gregg," they said in unison. "You're such a pain."

"Well, so are you two," sneered the blond-haired boy. "All you talk about is horses—yuk."

"Better than the dumb stuff you guys talk about," Penny shot back. She was tall enough to look right over the top of Gregg's head. She considered him a jerk and even more obnoxious than most of the boys in her class. Boys were definitely not a priority in either girl's life.

The ringing bell interrupted them. With relief Penny and Jan turned toward their homeroom door. "I'll talk to you later," Penny said to Jan. "Meet me by my bus after school."

Two

Bones was at the far side of the pasture and lifted his head as Penny and Jan hurried down Mr. Billings's drive later that afternoon. Penny called to him. Perhaps he remembered her voice from the day before, because he came trotting over.

"Well, here he is!" Penny beamed as she and Jan climbed through the rails of the fence.

"Hey there, boy," Penny said, holding out an apple on her palm. "Remember me? Meet my friend, Jan."

Bones nickered as if he understood, and Penny scratched behind his large ears. The two girls studied the animal as he munched down on the crisp apple. He certainly was a sorry sight, with the burrs and mud on his rough coat. At sixteen hands, his withers—the point where his neck sloped down to meet his back—reached above Penny's shoulder. His legs were long, but so furry it was difficult to see their shape. His bones were obvious at his withers and hips, where they protruded slightly, and when Penny ran her hand down his side, she could feel a few ribs.

Penny hadn't remembered him looking quite so shabby. "What do you think?" she asked slowly.

"I don't know . . ." Jan sounded a little doubtful.

11

But Penny was determined. "Come on," she said to her friend. "Let's go to the barn and get some brushes. He'll look a lot better cleaned up. There's an old halter and lead rope, too."

Bones lazily followed along, curious and hoping for another apple.

Jan held the brushes while Penny took down the dusty halter and lead rope. Penny brushed the worst of the dirt off both with an old rag, then the two girls returned to the pasture where Bones was waiting.

Penny fed him another apple, then looped the lead rope around his neck. While he was busy chewing, she slid the halter up over his nose and ears and buckled the cheek strap.

"We can tie him to the fence," Jan suggested, "and each of us take a side."

"That's what I was thinking," Penny said, leading the horse to the fence.

At first Bones didn't seem very happy about being tied. He shook his head as Penny got a currycomb from Jan and walked around him. But once the girls set to work, he immediately quieted down.

"He likes it!" Penny smiled.

"Most horses do," Jan answered. "Don't *you* like your back scratched?"

Penny worked the currycomb in a circular motion, allowing the short teeth of the round comb to pick up loose hair and dirt. The remains of Bones's heavy winter coat came out in clumps. Every few minutes she had to stop and clean the comb. She worked the comb down his neck, over his shoulders, then along his back and his side.

"He's looking better already," Jan called over the horse's back.

"I don't believe the difference!" Penny was growing more and more excited. "I can't wait to see him when we're finished. I should have brought a camera and taken before and after pictures."

When the worst of the dried mud and loose hair had been curried away, the girls applied soft-bristled brushes to Bones's dark bay coat. The brushing got rid of the lighter dirt and brought up a dull shine. Penny then went to work on his tangled mane and tail.

An hour later, she and Jan stepped back to admire their efforts.

"Not bad!" Jan grinned. "He's still going to need a lot more grooming, but this is a good start. He looks like a different horse."

Penny's smile was so wide, she could hardly speak. She rubbed Bones's nose. "I'll need to get a hoof pick, won't I, even though he's not shod?"

"You should. I've got an extra one at the stable. He's going to have to have shoes, though, if you're ever going to take him out on harder ground."

For the first time, a frown marked Penny's face. "And I need a saddle and bridle, too. How am I going to get enough money?"

"Don't worry about it yet," Jan said. "People are always advertising used tack for sale at the stable. I could probably find you something not too expensive."

Penny immediately perked up. "Do you think so?"

"I have a lesson tomorrow. I'll check. Now that he's groomed, let's see how he looks. Walk him around the pasture." Jan climbed up and sat on the top rail of the fence for a better view.

Penny untied Bones and started leading him away at a walk. She circled the pasture. Bones followed along without protest.

"Now trot him," Jan called.

Penny tugged on the lead rope and started off at a jog. She was stopped short in her tracks by Bones. He wouldn't increase his speed above a walk. He gazed at her stubbornly as she turned around.

"Don't let him get away with that!" Jan yelled. "He's just being lazy. Turn him in a circle and try it again!"

Penny did, and after several tries, Bones finally gave in and picked up his pace to a slow trot. Penny kept him going around the pasture, and for good measure, took him around a second time. She patted his neck when they came to a stop beside Jan.

"Good boy!"

"He looks sound." Jan jumped down from the fence. "And he's got nice movement, but he's going to need *a lot* of training. He's too used to being lazy and doing exactly what he wants."

"Do you think I can make a jumper out of him?"

"Too soon to tell. First you've got to get him used to having a saddle on his back."

"I've got an awful lot of work ahead."

"But think what fun you're going to have!" Jan laughed.

Penny nodded happily. She couldn't wait! She hated to leave the horse and go home, but it was five o'clock already. She unclipped the lead rope and watched as Bones meandered off to a patch of fresh, green grass.

"After all our work," she teased, "I bet he'll go right out and roll in the mud."

The girls collected the brushes and brought them back to the barn. They talked over Penny's plans for the horse. Bones definitely needed fattening up, and with some grain in his diet, he'd probably be more spirited, too. With Jan's help, Penny would then start training him on a longe line. Walking and trotting him around the pasture would help condition his muscles.

When they came out of the barn, Mr. Billings was leaning against the fence.

"So, you decided to give it a try, eh?" he said.

Penny felt a moment's panic. "It's still all right, isn't it?"

"Can't see any harm in it." The old man studied the horse. "Cleaned him up some. I hardly recognized him."

"This is my friend Jan, Mr. Billings. She's going to come over sometimes to help me out."

Mr. Billings nodded to the other girl. "Fine with me, but, like I said, I wouldn't get my hopes up." He turned and started back to his house.

On Saturday morning, Penny volunteered to go shopping with her mother. Normally she hated shopping, but the feed store was right around the corner from the supermarket. She'd carefully counted out her savings and had put ten dollars in her pocket before leaving the house.

During the drive into town, Penny hesitantly brought up the subject of the old horse and her plans for him. Her mother listened patiently, then smiled.

"Is that where you and Jan were the other afternoon? I thought you might be cooking something up."

"Please, Mom, can I do it? It won't cost you anything, like riding lessons would, and I'll pay for anything extra I need out of the money I've saved."

Her mother thought it over for a minute. "Yes, I guess it's all right, as long as you have Mr. Billings's permission. But I don't want you neglecting your homework and the things you're supposed to do around the house."

"I won't—I promise!"

When they arrived at the supermarket, Penny shot off to the feed store. She'd never bought grain before and had no idea of its cost. As she walked down the aisle and studied the prices, she had a shock. Her ten dollars would only buy enough grain for a couple of weeks. Her savings would be gone in no time at all, and she still had to buy a saddle and bridle and eventually pay for shoeing!

Resignedly she handed over her ten dollars in exchange for a much smaller package than she'd imagined and left the store.

Back at home she rushed through her chores. She unpacked the groceries, emptied the dishwasher, and straightened her room. Then she got ready to see Bones. She'd found some ragged towels and an old, moth-eaten blanket in the bottom of the linen closet the night before. With those under one arm, the sack of grain under the other, and apples filling her jacket pockets, she headed off for Mr. Billings's. Bones had been doing well on the longe line the last few days, and Penny was already planning the next step in his training.

First she scooped a few handfuls of grain into a bucket and brought it out to the horse. As he smelled the grain, his nostrils quivered and he pricked his ears. He eagerly shoved his nose into the bucket. In no time at all, he'd licked the bucket clean and was nosing around on the ground for fallen bits. He lifted his head and gazed expectantly at Penny.

"You'll get some more later," she said, laughing, "but only if you're good."

She brought out the brushes from the barn and groomed him. He'd been rolling in the mud again, but with the worst of his winter coat curried away, the mud brushed off easily. Next she attached the lead line to his halter and walked and trotted him around the pasture. The grain couldn't have helped already, so maybe he was beginning to understand what was expected of him. He trotted beside her more energetically than he had the day before.

After several laps, Penny decided to try her next plan. She got out the old blanket, folded it to approximately saddle size and laid it on his back. Bones let it rest for a moment, then he rippled his back muscles, trying to knock it off. When that didn't work, he screwed his head around, gripped the edge of the blanket in his teeth, and pulled it off.

17

"You're a smart old guy, aren't you?" Penny chuckled. She retrieved the blanket and went through the same routine over and over, until Bones resigned himself to the light pressure on his back and let the blanket stay. Feeling proud of her progress, Penny walked him around with the blanket, then trotted him. She was tempted to bring him over to the fence and try lowering her own weight onto his back, but knew that would be pushing things too fast.

Instead, she tied Bones to the fence and went out behind the pasture where Mr. Billings had piled some large broken branches. She selected five that were straight and the size of poles. Then she dragged them back to the pasture and set them out in parallel rows several feet apart. Untying Bones, she led him toward the branches. The object was to get him to walk over the poles and not on them.

At first he tried to walk around them altogether. Penny refused to let him get away with it. At last he walked down the middle, carefully lifting his hooves over each of the obstacles. Penny rewarded him with a piece of apple, and Bones seemed to decide this wasn't so bad after all. She walked him through several times.

Next she led him through at a trot. His hooves rapped a couple of the branches the first time. Penny didn't give him an apple. The horse snorted in disgust, but the next time through, he lifted his feet more carefully. He trotted briskly over every obstacle and finally got his reward.

Penny was thrilled with their progress but she didn't want to tire Bones out. She took off the halter and lead line, then headed for the barn.

She spent the rest of the afternoon cleaning out the corner of the barn near Bones's stall. She took a broom to the cobwebs on the ceiling. Then she dusted off the shelf and carefully laid out all of her grooming aids. She sorted through the old trunk and rearranged its contents. She washed out all the buckets and stacked them neatly. Finally she swept the old floor boards and removed many years' worth of dirt. She was sneezing by the time she stepped outside, but the barn looked a hundred percent better.

Penny was feeling very satisfied when she headed home at five o'clock. She'd barely gotten into the house when the phone rang. It was Jan.

"I've got the best news," Jan said excitedly. "I've found you a saddle and a bridle!"

"You have? Oh, wow!" Penny plopped down in a kitchen chair.

"I've seen them, too. They look okay—pretty dirty—but cheap. They belong to a girl who quit riding. Her parents just want to get rid of her gear. They'll even throw in an old saddle pad if they can sell them right away. I told the stable guy to hold them for you."

"How much?"

"Seventy-five dollars."

"I can just afford it, but I'm going to have to do some baby-sitting to earn more money for grain and other supplies. When can I get them?"

"I talked to my mother. She said we could pick them up tomorrow when I have my lesson. She'll pay for them, and you can give her back the money

19

when we drop the stuff off. Should we bring them over to Mr. Billings's? My lesson's over at three."

"I'll be there," Penny said, grinning.

That night after dinner, Penny sat down with pencil and paper and figured out how much money she'd have left in her special savings after she bought the saddle and bridle. There was no way around it. She was going to have to take on several evening baby-sitting jobs a week, plus take care of Bones, and do her homework. But it was worth it. Penny lay back on her bed and imagined herself riding Bones around the pasture. She fell asleep with a smile on her lips.

Three

Within another week's time Bones was looking much more fit. The grain had helped fill up his hollows, and the grooming had brought a deep sheen to his coat. He was friskier, too, but not always to Penny's advantage. Before, he'd simply been lazy. Now, he exerted his will with a new stubbornness. Yet he knew Penny on sight and gave a delighted whinny when she arrived at Mr. Billings's with Jan the following Sunday morning.

Penny wrapped her arms around Bones's neck and gave him a big squeeze. Then she went to the barn, collected her saddle, bridle, and a brush, and brought them out to the pasture fence.

"Hey," Jan said, "that tack looks almost new. You've been busy with the saddle soap."

"For nearly an hour. The tack was really dirty. The girl who had it couldn't have cleaned it very often."

"She wasn't very interested in riding. I think her parents pushed her into it."

"I wish my parents had more interest," Penny said sadly. She laid the saddle over the fence rail and hooked the lead rope to Bones's halter. But soon she was smiling again as she picked up the brush and ran it over Bones's coat. She'd spent the last few days getting Bones used to the saddle on his back, and

21

she couldn't wait to show Jan. "He sure can be stubborn when he wants to," she told Jan. "I hope he doesn't try any tricks today."

Penny lifted the saddle from the fence. Bones flattened his ears for an instant, and he tensed his muscles. Penny ran a gentle hand down his neck and spoke soothingly to him. "That's a good boy. It's okay. Let's show Jan how far we've gotten."

At her tone and soft touch, Bones relaxed. Penny brought the girth around under his belly and carefully fastened the buckles. She left them loose enough so that Bones didn't feel any sudden pinching. She then picked up the bridle, dropped the reins over his head and loosened his halter. Using the reins around his neck to hold him, she slid off his halter and quickly positioned the bridle, drawing it over his muzzle. He was used to the bridle and bit from his days pulling a cart. He opened his mouth and accepted the bit. Penny slid the bridle up over his ears and buckled the throat-latch.

Penny turned and grinned at Jan, who gave her a thumbs-up sign. "Now watch this," Penny said. With the reins securely tied behind Bones's neck, Penny clipped a long lead line to the bridle and led Bones forward. They walked and trotted the circuit of the pasture, then Penny led him toward the poles set out on the grass about four feet apart and trotted him through. He lifted his feet cleanly and smoothly.

"Great," Jan called. "He's getting *much* better. Let's raise the poles and make cavalletti."

Real cavalletti would consist of a series of poles, supported at each end by X-shaped brackets, spaced about four or five feet apart and raised about six inches above the ground. Trotting or cantering over them would strengthen a horse's legs and help his coordination. Penny and Jan figured they could find enough materials around the farm to make their own cavalletti.

Penny tied Bones, and the two girls scurried around near the barn looking for bricks or blocks of wood—anything they could place under the ends of the poles to raise them several inches off the ground. They found several fireplace logs and a few bricks. They inserted them under the ends of the poles until the poles were secure and fairly level.

"Okay, let him get a good look at it first," Jan said, "then trot him through."

Penny led Bones up the side of their improvised cavalletti. They'd spaced the poles so that Bones could trot over one with each stride taken. Several yards in front of the first pole, she turned him, let him have a good look, then trotted him forward. He trotted without hesitation, but a few feet in front of the first pole he suddenly realized these poles were different from the last group he'd trotted through. He stopped dead in his tracks.

Penny immediately turned him and repeated the exercise, keeping firm pressure on the lead line. The horse began to hesitate, but she urged him forward with her voice. "Come on, Bones, this is easy. You can do it."

The horse continued forward over the first pole, clipping it with his hoof. He immediately lifted his feet higher as he trotted over the rest of the poles.

"Good boy!" Penny told him as she trotted him back to the start.

His ears perked, and he lifted his head a little higher. He was enjoying this new game and was eager as Penny trotted him back for several more tries. The last time through, he actually hopped over the obstacles.

"Did you see that?" Penny laughed as she walked Bones back to the pasture fence. "He was trying to jump."

"He sure seemed to like it," Jan said, coming over to rub the old horse's neck as Penny gave him a bit of apple for his reward. "Won't Mr. Billings be surprised!"

"I think Bones is feeling pretty proud of himself, too." The old horse certainly did seem to be holding himself more smartly. "I was going to try sitting in the saddle today," Penny said, considering. "What do you think, Jan? Is it too soon?"

Jan thought it over. "We can try. You can take him to the middle of the pasture and I'll hold him for you. But first, put on that old hard hat I brought."

Bones stood patiently as Jan held his lead and Penny secured the hat. Penny then carefully tightened the saddle girth.

"Just try leaning your weight over the saddle," Jan instructed her.

Penny carefully lowered the left stirrup. Standing close to the horse's left shoulder and facing the rear, she placed her left hand on Bones's neck and put her left foot in the stirrup. Although Penny had little experience in the saddle, she'd memorized every instruction in her riding books. Of course, reading about riding and actually doing it were two different things. She was a little nervous as she reached across Bones's saddle with her right hand and slowly lifted her weight onto the foot in the stirrup.

Bones immediately reacted. He sidestepped, pranced, and turned his body around. Penny's grip wasn't firm enough. She went over backwards. Her foot slipped from the stirrup, and she landed on her backside on the grass.

"Try again," Jan said before Penny had even gotten back on her feet. "You have to let him know who's boss."

Jan soothed Bones, and Penny tried again, this time gripping Bones's mane with her fingers. It didn't hurt the horse, she knew, and it gave her more security. She was prepared for his side-stepping this time and managed to hold on and lean her weight over his back as he danced in circles around Jan.

Bones didn't like what was going on one bit. "Easy, boy, easy," Penny crooned. The horse snorted and pranced and arched his back. Penny stayed glued to the saddle. Her stomach was balanced over the seat of the saddle—not the most elegant of positions! But she kept talking to Bones. For an instant he quieted and she started to relax. Then he rocketed into his dancing act again. Penny held on for dear life, while Jan soothed the horse.

"Easy . . . easy . . . it's okay, boy."

Penny's stomach muscles could take no more, and she was sure she was going to slide to the ground. Unexpectedly Bones quieted, then stood still. He craned his head around to the right and looked at Penny where she hung over the saddle.

"It's just me, boy." She tried to smile. "No one's going to hurt you."

He snorted, but remained quiet.

"Bring your leg over," Jan said softly.

"But the other stirrup's not down!" Penny whispered back.

"Hold on with your leg. I think he's gotten used to the weight."

Penny straightened up. Bones was still eyeing her. Slowly she lifted her right leg and swung it up over the saddle. She eased into a sitting position and cautiously settled her weight into the saddle. "Whew," she whispered.

But Bones had other ideas. He snorted explosively, arched his back, and gave a tremendous buck. Penny was taken completely by surprise. She lost her one stirrup and a second later went flying off to land in the mud. Nothing but her pride was hurt, but she was getting angry. When she got to her feet and turned around, Jan was laughing.

"Are you okay? I'm sorry . . . but you look so funny with mud all over your face"—Jan giggled—"you might as well learn how to fall right from the start. It won't be the first time."

Penny stuck out her tongue at Jan and glowered at Bones. "You think you're going to get off that easy, do you?" The horse looked back at her mildly, as if he didn't know what she was talking about. Penny went to his right side and pulled down the stirrup. Then she marched around and prepared to mount again.

Jan had stopped giggling and offered some suggestions. "Once you're on, sink your heels down. Keep the stirrup irons under the balls of your feet. Hold on with your legs, but don't squeeze him, and get a good grip on his mane."

Penny nodded. Her light brown eyes were narrowed in determination. Bones's ears flicked back and forth as he waited. Penny mounted quickly and shoved her foot immediately into the right stirrup. Bones stood totally still for a moment. Then he erupted into a series of quick, jerking bucks. Penny gripped his mane in both hands and wrapped her legs around his sides. She wasn't going to fall off this time if she could help it.

She had several shaky moments. Bones cavorted, twisted his body, kicked out, and danced in a circle around Jan. But Penny's determination to stay on was greater than his ability to get her off. His efforts to unseat her became less frantic. They slowed down and then finally stopped. He continued to prance in nervous circles around Jan, though, who held firmly to the lead. Finally he quivered to a halt and let out a shuddering huff of resignation.

Penny immediately rubbed his neck. "Good boy . . . good boy! See, this isn't so bad."

Bones twitched his muscles and rolled his eyes unhappily. Penny continued to reassure him. His ears flicked around as he listened to her voice. After several minutes, he relaxed. Penny expelled the breath she'd been holding.

"As long as we've gone this far," Jan said quietly, "I'm going to lead him around at a walk. You all set?"

Penny nodded. At Jan's gentle encouragement, Bones moved slowly forward. His ears constantly flicked back to Penny as she continued to talk to him softly. They made their way around the pasture. On their second trip around, Penny picked up the reins. With her thumbs pointing up, she fed the reins between her fourth fingers and pinkies, then up along her palms. Since Jan was leading Bones, there was no need for Penny to exert any pressure, but she was able to get a feel for what it would be like on her own.

When both girls were sure Bones had accepted Penny in the saddle and wouldn't be doing anything unexpected, Jan relaxed the pressure on the lead rope.

"Try to get him to move forward by yourself," Jan suggested. "Hold the reins just in front of the saddle—but don't pull on them. Squeeze a little with your legs and shift your weight forward a little bit."

Penny did. Bones hesitated an instant, then walked forward.

"Keep your heels down," Jan added. "Your toes should point up, and you should feel the muscles in the back of your calves stretch. And sit up straight."

"Aye, aye, sir!" Penny said, laughing.

Penny remembered all of those instructions from her few riding experiences. Doing everything

28

correctly at the same time was more difficult. When she concentrated on keeping her heels down, her hands moved out of position. When she concentrated on straightening her shoulders and head, her heels popped up. Jan walked around with her twice, then unclipped the lead.

"Try it on your own. When you want him to stop, lean back slightly in the saddle and pull *gently* on the reins. When he stops, release the pressure."

Penny licked her lips and set off. To her amazement, she and Bones did fine. Of course, he knew the circuit around the pasture by now. There was no need for her to direct him to turn, but the fact that she was actually riding him was enough to make her face glow.

As she finished her third circle, she saw Mr. Billings come over to the fence and stand beside Jan. She suddenly remembered that she hadn't asked for Mr. Billings's permission to ride. What if he wouldn't let her work with Bones anymore?

Penny stopped Bones in front of them and dismounted. She brought the reins over Bones's head and gave him a huge hug around the neck. The horse nuzzled her shoulder.

Penny turned to face Mr. Billings. "Is it all right?" she asked worriedly. "I mean, riding him?"

"Didn't think you could do it," Mr. Billings said with a hint of a smile. "But, yup, I suppose it's okay. Guess you're never too old to learn."

Hearing his owner's voice, Bones stretched his head toward the old man. "Guess you deserve some credit yourself, old boy." Mr. Billings reached in his pocket and extracted a sugar cube. "Only because it's a special occasion. Don't want you getting spoiled."

Bones lipped up the sugar and munched happily as Mr. Billings rubbed his head.

"Been watching you through the window this week," Mr. Billings said to Penny. "Admire your persistence. I left something in the barn for you, inside the stall."

Penny gave him a puzzled look. The old man seemed embarrassed, and shifted his feet. "Since you're making a new animal out of my horse, thought I'd help you out a bit. Well, go and look."

Penny handed the reins to Jan and hurried across to the barn. She couldn't imagine what Mr. Billings would have left her. When she peered inside the stall, she saw a one-hundred-pound sack of grain resting against the wood partition. It was enough food to last for most of the summer! Penny let out a whoop and went running back outside.

"Thank you, Mr. Billings! Thank you!"

But the old man had already started back to the house. He lifted his hand briefly in acknowledgment.

"It's one hundred pounds of grain," Penny told Jan excitedly. "I won't have to worry about finding the money for feed!"

"Wow!" Jan looked toward Mr. Billings's departing back. "That was nice of him."

Penny laughed and did a little dance along the pasture fence. "Bones is broken to saddle, and now

I'll have money for shoeing. Oh, Jan, I'm so excited! What a wonderful day!"

The girls gave each other a hug. Bones added his two cents by pushing his nose up against them and nickering.

Four

"Penny, are you with us? Can you give me the answer?"

Penny jerked her head around from the window and looked at her teacher. "I'm sorry, Miss Frazer. Could you repeat the question?"

"It's a beautiful day, and I know all of you would rather be outside enjoying it, but let's *try* to concentrate." Miss Frazer gave a small, understanding smile. "Can you tell me where George Washington took his first Presidential oath of office?"

"Yes, in New York," Penny answered quickly.

"Correct. Now, class, it's important . . ."

Penny tried to pay attention as Miss Frazer continued their year-end review, but her heart wasn't in it. She much preferred daydreaming about Bones and their progress together.

Penny had improved so much in her riding in just a few short weeks. She'd mastered the posting trot. She'd ridden Bones over the cavalletti and had started him doing figure eights around the pasture. Doing figure eights was good for both Penny and Bones because she got to practice giving commands to the horse. Bones learned to respond instantly to her commands and became more supple in the process.

That afternoon Penny planned to try him at a canter, but worried whether she'd remember all the things she was supposed to do with her hands and legs. Jan had a piano lesson after school and couldn't come with her.

Finally the dismissal bell rang. Penny flew out of the building to the school bus as if she had wings on her feet. At home she changed into jeans and a shirt, called to her mother that she'd be back at five-thirty, and set out for Mr. Billings's.

Bones nickered happily when he saw her. Penny groomed him carefully and cleaned his hooves, then gave him a big kiss on the nose. "You're getting so pretty! Do you know that? You're not an old nag anymore." He seemed to agree with her compliments and lifted his head a little higher.

Penny warmed them both up by going through all the paces they'd learned so far. She walked him around the pasture and mentally checked her seat and position in the saddle. Her back was straight, her shoulders square, and her head was up so that she looked over Bones's head between his ears. Her hands were in the correct position on the reins. She held them firmly with no unnecessary slack, yet not so tightly that she was pulling on Bones's mouth. Her heels were down in the stirrups with her toes pointing forward. As she approached the turns in the figure eight, she looked in the direction of the turn and, with her rein, inclined Bones's head very slightly toward it.

Satisfied that she was finally getting it all together, she took her feet from the stirrups and rode around again at a walk and trot using just her legs and body for balance. Then she put her feet back in the stirrups and urged Bones into a trot. She

33

still needed to practice posting—rising and sitting in the saddle in time with the movement of his legs. As they circled she watched his outside shoulder. When it rose, she rose in the saddle in rhythm with his stride. At the center of the figure eight, she sat an extra stride in the saddle, and as they circled in the opposite direction, she rose with his opposite shoulder, or on the opposite diagonal.

For their first attempt at a canter, she would take him in a wide oval, counterclockwise. To be properly balanced, Bones would have to lean slightly to his left on the turns. Penny knew that pulling gently on the right rein and pressing her left leg to his side would encourage Bones to use his left, or inside, leg to lead. Once he broke into a canter, she must sit straight and deep in the saddle, keep her hands and body steady, and flow with the rhythm of his pace. Could she remember all that? She'd never know until she tried.

Penny started Bones at a trot up the long side of their oval. As they approached the turn, she gathered the reins slightly. She sat down in the saddle, tightened one rein and pressed with her legs as she was supposed to. Bones continued trotting. She tried again, this time doing everything with more emphasis. Bones stubbornly continued at a trot. Penny didn't release the pressure of her legs and pulled harder on the outside rein. The horse snorted in frustration, but at last broke into a reluctant canter.

Penny could tell from the jerkiness of his stride that something was wrong. Bones seemed to be off balance. She pulled him back to a trot and tried

34

again. This time she got him off on the correct lead, but in concentrating on that, she allowed her head to drop and her hands to jog on the reins. Bones went back to a trot.

"Oh, darn it!" she cried in exasperation. But she tried again, and again, until she got it right. At last she had Bones cantering in merry circles around the pasture as she sat back and relaxed.

When she finally pulled him to a stop and dismounted, her legs felt like rubber and didn't want to support her. She stood for a second at Bones's side, shaking out each leg in turn, but she was still wobbly. She rested for a moment until she realized that the heavier exercise had brought up a sweat on Bones's coat. She untacked him and walked him around the pasture for a half hour to cool him out. After he'd cooled, she brushed him lightly again as a reward, cleaned his hooves, put away her tack and grooming materials, then fed him.

Penny leaned back against the fence and watched Bones dip contentedly into his bucket of grain. He looked so different now with a gleaming coat and no bones sticking out. He'd never pass for a Thoroughbred though. His ears were a little too large, and he was Roman-nosed. His legs seemed longer and more graceful now, but his body still seemed out of proportion because of his strong, heavy hindquarters. Of course, Penny knew the strong hindquarters would be an asset in jumping, and in her eyes, Bones *was* beautiful. That was all that mattered.

He looked up as if reading her mind, nickered softly, then stuck his nose back in the bucket. Penny smiled to herself. She felt very happy and very lucky.

Penny was exhausted by the time she got home. She headed straight for the bathroom, ran hot water into the tub, and stripped off her dirty clothes. Easing down under the hot water, she sighed. Her sore muscles needed this. She'd tried hard to hide her aches and pains from her family, but it wasn't always easy. In riding, she was exercising muscles she didn't normally use. Sometimes her muscles stiffened up overnight, and she could hardly stand up straight in the morning.

But she felt much better when she got out of the tub. She would have loved to curl up in bed after dinner with a good horse story, but she wouldn't have that luxury. She had to baby-sit for the Flanagans that night, plus do her homework.

Her parents seemed quieter than usual as the family sat down at the dinner table. She guessed that they were worrying about money again. Penny gave it no more thought, dug into her food with relish, and drifted off into her favorite daydream—Bones.

She looked up when she heard her father call her name. "Yes, Dad?" she said.

He cleared his throat before he spoke. "Your mother and I are concerned about you, Penny. It's about your schedule. Now that you've gotten so involved taking care of this horse, you're neglecting other, more important things."

Penny stared at him, dumbstruck.

"You're constantly on the go and wearing yourself out. That's not good for a growing girl."

"I'm fine, Dad. I don't mind being busy."

"Busy is one thing. Burning the candle at both ends is another. It's too much for you. You've gotten behind with your regular chores in the house, and we're afraid that your grades will start falling next."

"But I always make the honor roll," Penny protested.

"That was before you started spending all your time with this horse." Her father shifted in his chair, but Penny could see that he and her mother had already discussed it and made up their minds. "I'm all for having interests and hobbies. I certainly enjoy my fishing, but I don't put it before my job. Your mother and I have decided that you have to cut down on the time you spend at Mr. Billings's. A couple of days a week is more than enough. You can go over on the weekends and concentrate on your schoolwork during the week."

"But, Dad, Bones depends on me. He needs me more than just on weekends. He's doing so well—so am I. I'm learning to ride . . . I've never been *happier*!" Tears welled up in Penny's eyes. They couldn't mean it.

"Exercise is great," her father said, "but what are you going to *do* with the riding? We can't afford lessons for you, and by the time you can afford them for yourself, you'll have lost interest—"

"I won't lose interest, Dad, and I'm learning so much. I want to train Bones to jump. I know I can do it. We've learned so much together already."

"Penny, the horse doesn't even belong to you. You can't go making plans like that."

"Mr. Billings says it's okay."

"I didn't know you were jumping," Penny's mother put in. "That's dangerous."

"Well, we're not jumping yet. And besides, Jan's helping me. She's been taking lessons for *years*. We're not doing anything dangerous, and I've got a hard hat if I fall. Oh, please—it's *so* important to me."

Her parents exchanged a thoughtful look. Finally her father said, "We'll talk it over and let you know our decision later."

Penny nodded. She'd lost her appetite and only picked at her food until it was time to clear the table. Her younger brother, Jimmy followed her to the kitchen.

"What do you want to ride for? I think it's boring," he whispered as they filled the dishwasher.

"And I think all the fishing you do is boring. You're always tying those stupid flies and digging up worms and stuff."

"Fishing's different."

"You're right," Penny muttered. "Riding's a lot more exciting—if Mom and Dad don't stop me from doing it."

Jimmy considered. "I'll make a deal. I'll help out with a couple of your chores, so they think you're doing them . . ."

Penny eyed him suspiciously. "What do you want?"

"To use your cassette player and headphones when you're not home." He grinned impishly.

"Come on, Jimmy, every time you touch my stuff, you break it."

He only continued grinning.

"Oh, all right." Penny relented. "But you better stick to your half of the deal."

"I will. I promise."

Despite Jimmy's offer to help, Penny worried through the whole two hours she spent baby-sitting at the Flanagans'. She'd absolutely die if her parents decided she couldn't work with Bones every day. Weekends weren't enough. He might forget everything she'd taught him in between, and besides, he'd miss her—just like she'd miss him.

She practiced her riding exercises as a means of distraction. Standing with her toes on the edge of a stair tread, she lowered her heels as far as they would go and bounced several times lightly. The exercise helped stretch the muscles along the back of her calves. Then she sat on a stool. Extending her arms out to either side, she turned at the waist, all the way to the right, then all the way to the left, keeping her lower body still. She followed this with large arm circles. The object again was to keep her lower body perfectly stationary.

Penny's exercises went fine, but her stomach felt like it was tied in a knot when Mr. Flanagan dropped her back home. She found her parents in the living room.

"Well," her father said when he saw her come in. "We've talked it over, Penny. Since it's so close to the end of the school year, you can continue on with the horse through the summer. But as soon as school starts, you'll have to limit your time with the horse to weekends and concentrate on your studies. We're not trying to be mean, but your education's a lot more important now."

Penny barely heard her father's last words. She ran across the room and gave both her mother and father a hug. "Thank you! You won't be sorry. Wait till you see how good we are!"

Later, when Penny's initial excitement had worn off, she remembered her parents' deadline. The end of summer. Those months of vacation seemed to stretch lazily into the distance, but Penny knew from experience how quickly they'd actually speed by. She couldn't face the thought of practically giving up Bones when school started again.

What could she do to convince her parents how important riding was to her—not just for the summer, but always?

Five

"I've got it!" Jan said. She lifted her chin off her clasped hands. Her blue eyes were shining with inspiration. "You and Bones are going to enter a jumping division at the end-of-summer show and take a first!"

The two girls were sitting on the sunny lawn behind the school, eating their lunches and talking over Penny's problem.

"Just like that?" Penny said, her eyes wide.

"Well, your parents are bound to notice that! Then they'd *have* to let you keep riding!"

"Maybe . . . But Jan, we haven't even started jumping yet. What if Bones doesn't like it?"

"Oh, he will. Any horse will jump. Some are just better than others."

"Do you really think I could get good enough to win a blue ribbon by the end of summer?" Penny wanted to believe it was possible, but it seemed like an awful lot to accomplish over a few short months.

"If you try hard enough," Jan answered. Her expression was lively. "You're a natural at riding."

"I am?"

"You're picking it up faster than I did when I started."

"I guess that's because I've dreamed about riding for so long." Penny dropped the remains of

41

her sandwich in her brown paper bag and pulled out a packet of cookies. "Yuk, oatmeal."

"I'll trade you," Jan said, handing over some chocolate-chip cookies.

As Penny started unwrapping the cookies, she suddenly grinned. "Of course! Winning a blue ribbon is *exactly* what I need to do . . . and I won't know unless I try! You're not teasing, Jan? You *really* think we could do it?"

"I know we can! It's going to mean a lot of work, though. You're going to have to start training Bones over jumps right away."

"And training me, too." Penny laughed, feeling a tingle of excitement. "If we started today . . ."

For the rest of the lunch break, the girls talked about crossbars, low fences, and hunt and jump seats.

That afternoon at Mr. Billings's, Jan sat on the fence coaching, and Penny started practicing the jump seat.

"That's it," Jan called. "Keep your weight back in your heels. Lift slightly out of the saddle. Lean very slightly forward—shoulders square, back slightly arched, head up. Right! Keep going. Trot around in a couple of circles. Now go over the poles."

Penny concentrated on what Jan had just told her as she and Bones approached the poles laid flat on the ground. Over they went. Bones extended his trotting stride slightly. The horse was enjoying himself as much as Penny was.

From the poles, they progressed to the cavalletti. Bones easily trotted over the slightly raised obstacles. She took Bones through several more times, until she felt confident and comfortable and knew what to expect.

"We should try a crossbar next, shouldn't we?" she called to Jan.

Jan nodded. "I was just wondering how we could set one up."

Penny dismounted and brought Bones to the rail. "How about a couple of cement blocks? I saw some in the barn."

"Good idea," Jan said as the two girls started across the pasture.

The blocks were heavy, but the girls managed to get them out to a level spot in the pasture and brace the end of a pole against each of the blocks to form an "X" in the middle.

Hands on her hips, Penny studied their handiwork. "I hope Mr. Billings doesn't mind us dragging all this stuff out here. I better talk to him before we leave and explain."

"We've got to build some bigger jumps eventually, too," Jan said.

"Mmmm, I've been thinking about that. I'll figure something out." But there was a tiny frown of worry on Penny's forehead as she remounted and gathered the reins. "I should approach at a trot, just like the cavalletti?"

"Right." Jan nodded.

Penny let Bones get a good look at the crossbar, then trotted him in a wide half-circle and approached the jump. She concentrated on getting her jump seat just right. Without the slightest hesitation, Bones popped over, leaving plenty of room to spare between his hooves and the poles.

Penny had her first experience with a jump, small though it was, and she quickly discovered the importance of perfect balance in the saddle.

"Hey, not bad!" Jan grinned.

Penny was delighted. She'd thought it was going to take a lot more work to convince Bones to jump. But he hadn't needed convincing. With the slightest pressure of her legs, over he'd gone. She took him over again, then Jan removed one pole and raised the end of the other so that it rested horizontally across the top of both blocks about a foot off the ground. Bones jumped over without blinking an eye. Penny was grinning from ear to ear.

"Try it at a canter," Jan suggested.

As Penny put Bones to a canter and circled around, she focused her eyes on the upcoming jump. It was harder to gauge her approach at the faster pace. She knew the importance of the approach and checking the horse's stride to prevent too early or too late a takeoff.

Penny raised into her jump seat, and again Bones cleared the obstacle without effort. Penny could tell he was excited by it all when he cantered off around the pasture. She had to pull him back to get him to slow down.

Twice more over the jump, and Penny decided they were ready for more. "Watch this!" she cried to Jan. She brought Bones around the pasture at a trot and reined him toward the cavalletti. He went through easily, but Penny wasn't finished. Urging him into a canter, she turned him at the end of the pasture and headed back to the single jump. They hopped over, and Bones seemed eager for more.

Penny trotted over to Jan. "Pretty good, huh?"

"You're not kidding." Jan was shaking her head. "Do you know, in less than an hour you've done three lessons' worth at the stable?"

"Really!" Penny patted Bones's neck. "You're doing good, old boy. But we're not finished yet, are we?" Her eyes were sparkling as she looked at Jan. "Let's set up one more jump after the cavalletti and the bar—and just a little higher."

"Are you sure?" Jan said doubtfully.

"Positive," Penny answered.

"Okay. But what are we going to use?"

Mr. Billings came strolling over to the pasture just then. He nodded to the girls. "You're doing all right there, Missy. I've been watching you. That old horse of mine is full of surprises."

"Thanks, Mr. Billings." Penny beamed. "He's great, isn't he? We were going to try him over one more fence—three in a row—but we weren't sure what we could use to build it."

The old man rubbed his chin thoughtfully. "I believe I can help you out." He disappeared behind his house, and returned in a minute carrying two round metal drums, one under each arm. "Empty kerosene cans from my stove," he explained. "They ought to do for the ends. I've got an old section of white gate you can rest against them."

He carried the drums into the pasture. "Where do you want 'em?"

Penny and Jan indicated the spot, and he set them down. Each stood about two and one-half feet high. The peeling white gate which Mr. Billings brought over next was about the same height.

"I don't know." Jan frowned. "That might be a little high for Bones the first time around. The single bar is only a foot off the ground."

"He can do it," Penny said confidently, rubbing Bones's nose. "Can't you, boy?"

Bones had been eyeing their newly constructed fence with curiosity. He rubbed his muzzle against Penny's shoulder as if to say that he could. Penny mounted.

"Remember," Jan said, coaching her, "you're going to need more leg going over the higher jump, and be prepared. *You're* going to feel it more, too."

Nodding, but feeling perfectly confident, Penny set off. Jan and Mr. Billings stood behind the pasture fence to watch as she trotted Bones around toward the cavalletti. They flitted over the poles as if Bones were floating on air and continued at a canter toward the bar. Bones popped over it with a smooth surge and cantered on toward the new fence. It was going so easily that Penny felt no qualms whatsoever until they were almost at the fence. She felt Bones hesitate, pull back. He sat back on his hindquarters. But Penny continued moving forward, over Bones's shoulder and the fence, and landed in a heap at the other side. Before she rolled, out of the corner of her eye she saw Bones come flying over the fence and land cleanly on the other side.

Within seconds Penny had brushed herself off and was back on her feet. Bones had gone on to canter around the pasture by himself, shaking his head in glee.

Both Jan and Mr. Billings hurried over to Penny. "Are you okay?" they asked in unison.

Penny nodded and blushed in embarrassment.

"You didn't prepare him properly," Jan said. "He was a half-stride off, coming to the fence."

"That's what I get for being cocky."

"Don't worry—everybody gets a dose of it," Jan said sympathetically. "I did. But did you see how he recovered and got himself over? That takes heart. He's a natural. He *wants* to jump."

"You mean another horse would have just stood there?" Penny turned to study Bones with new appreciation. He'd decided to rejoin them and was trotting over.

"Most horses would. I've had them do it to me. It's usually the rider's fault when a horse refuses a jump, but for a horse to make up for it and try to jump anyway—pretty good."

Mr. Billings tried to hide his smile with his hand. Bones came over and gave his master a nudge with his nose. "Think you're something, don't you?" Mr. Billings chuckled.

"Well," Penny said, brushing off her hands on the seat of her pants and straightening her hard hat, "I guess I should get right back up and try it again."

"Right," said Jan.

Penny remounted. Bones pricked his ears in readiness. This time Penny wasn't going to let her confidence get the better of her. She was alert and in control as she set out once more. Through the cavalletti, over the bar. She was really concentrating now. Bones had been a half-stride off the last time. She had to shorten his stride and give him a little more room. She gathered the reins and collected him. For some reason this seemed natural to Penny as she felt Bones's muscles bunching beneath her. She concentrated on the take-off point, yet focused her eyes over and beyond the jump as they approached. She gathered Bones a bit more, and at exactly the right moment squeezed lightly with her legs. Bones lifted into the air. They arrived at the other side of the fence together and intact as Bones smoothly cantered off.

Penny reined him in a circle, then brought him back to the pasture rail. Only then did she relax and let out a long, relieved breath.

"That's the way!" Jan was nodding her head. "Great."

"I should try it again," Penny said.

"Once more, but then stop before you both get tired," Jan said. "My riding teacher is always telling us to 'quit on a positive note.'"

"Makes sense." And Penny had to admit that she was starting to feel tired. But she pushed that tiredness away and concentrated on one more good round, which she and Bones managed with flying colors.

"Whew!" Penny sighed as she jumped to the ground. "Boy, do I feel like I've accomplished something today." She began to lead Bones around the pasture at a walk to cool him out.

"Well, you did," Jan agreed. She and Mr. Billings helped Penny untack Bones when she had finished walking him.

"He deserves a good grooming tonight, and an extra treat." Penny snuggled her head against Bones's neck.

"Don't worry about the treats," Mr. Billings said. He was already feeding Bones a couple of carrots. While the girls started grooming the horse, Mr. Billings walked out across the pasture and removed some of their improvised jumps.

"No point in him tripping over them in the night," he said. "We can set them up again to-morrow."

"'We?'" Penny and Jan looked at each other. Was Mr. Billings going to help them turn Bones into a champion?

Six

Penny arrived at Mr. Billings's the next afternoon to find a whole collection of things piled along the outside of the pasture fence. There were old barrels, wide boards, and fence posts.

Mr. Billings wasn't in sight, so Penny went up to his door and knocked. "Did you put out all those things for us?" she asked when he came to the door.

"Old junk anyway," he answered. "Maybe you can make some use of it."

"But how did you know what kind of jumps we'd need?"

"A little imagination is all. I've seen this jumping stuff on the TV and in magazines. Not that I paid much attention. Here by yourself today, are you?"

Penny nodded.

"If you need a hand, then, setting up, just yell. I can rig those poles to stand upright and fix something to set the boards on."

"That's really nice of you, Mr. Billings!"

He shrugged. "Don't have much else to do. Keeps me from being bored." As Penny hesitated on his doorstep, he waved his hand. "Well, go on. Get to it. The old nag's waiting."

Penny scurried off, shaking her head. Mr. Billings had turned out to be really nice!

She spent the afternoon going over everything she and Bones had done the day before. She'd decided that the best plan for her and Bones was to spend one day learning, and the next day getting it down pat. Tomorrow she would set up the new jumps.

They did well that day. Penny never let her concentration slip—even over the simplest exercise. She was learning that everything was important. If she intended to compete in a show by the end of summer, she and Bones had to be perfect.

The old horse didn't seem to mind. He liked it more and more, and Penny noticed what a difference the daily workout was making in him. His muscles had gained tone; he was more alert and interested, with ears pricked and eyes bright. His movements were faster and more supple; his legs seemed to have acquired springs. He could trot in smaller and smaller circles and figure eights, bending his body, changing his leads. Penny began to realize that all he'd needed to show his talent was someone who cared and gave him attention.

Bones didn't seem the least bit tired when Penny quit that afternoon, untacked, and groomed him. She wasn't tired either and would have kept riding till dark, but she had final exams the next day and had to go home to study. Four more days, then summer vacation. She couldn't wait!

Penny whistled off-key as she groomed Bones the next afternoon. She'd done well on her math final—the hardest class she had. Before tacking up, Penny examined the pile of materials Mr. Billings had left. The huge wooden barrels could be a big help in teaching Bones to jump obstacles that were both high and wide. There would be wide jumps in any show competition. Penny started rolling them toward the gate. They were heavier than she'd thought they would be. She did all right until she tried to maneuver them into the pasture. There was a small hump in the ground. She heaved and got nowhere, except that her feet slid out from under her on the grass.

"Need a hand?" Mr. Billings had come up beside her. "Two working's always easier than one," he said, and put his hands to the barrel's side.

In no time they had it in position along the pasture fence. They went back to get the other. They rolled the second barrel into place. Both barrels were on their sides, end to end. Mr. Billings rubbed his chin. "You'll be needing some fancier jumps than this," he mused. "They've got these brush jumps and uprights and false stone walls—not that I couldn't show you some real stone ones to jump over, just behind the pasture, but it's too overgrown."

"How do you know about all the jumps?" Penny asked, staring up at Mr. Billings in surprise.

He looked away and mumbled, "Drove up to town today. Got a couple of books from the library. They look simple to build . . . just don't know how you're going to get that old nag of mine to jump over them. Then again, you've been doing pretty good so far."

"Oh, we'll do even better, Mr. Billings!" Penny said eagerly. "We're going to enter an end-of-summer horse show—if it's okay with you. Bones and I are going to win the blue ribbon!"

"Are you?" Mr. Billings's eyes twinkled. "Really think you can do it?"

"I'm going to try," Penny said with determination. She decided to confide in Mr. Billings. "You see, my parents want me to stop coming over here—except on weekends. They don't understand. They're worried about schoolwork, but I always make the honor roll. They don't realize that it's *important* to me to ride and have a horse." Penny looked down momentarily at her feet. "Of course, it's expensive to take regular lessons at a stable, and they don't have a lot of money. That's why it's so important for me to work with Bones. I want to do something with horses for the rest of my life!" Penny stared at him with defiant eyes. She waited for him to tell her, like most grown-ups did, that it was only a dream.

Mr. Billings didn't. He laughed, and patted her on the shoulder. "Well, let's get out there and show them. Don't know when I've seen such spirit. My daughters didn't have it . . . and not my granddaughters, either." He seemed a little sad for a moment, then pushed her off toward Bones. "What fences do you need? I'll help you build them."

"They've got to be fairly low for now," Penny answered, "so the kind where we can raise the poles would be great."

Mr. Billings nodded, then told Penny to wait a minute. He went to the house and returned with a large book in his hand. He opened it to some photos and drawings. "Like these?" he asked.

"Just like those," Penny answered excitedly.

First they put up an improvised brush jump to familiarize Bones with jumping over greenery. Mr. Billings had a large accumulation of brush around his property and Penny broke off several armloads of leafy branches. Then Mr. Billings got out a hammer, nails, and a handsaw. He pulled two fence posts and some old boards from the pile, made some quick measurements, and began sawing.

Penny leaned on the fence, watching him. "What are you doing?"

"Making some bases for these posts so they'll stand by themselves. Then I'll nail on some supports to hold the poles. Won't look very fancy, but it should work."

The new fence did work fine. They set it up between the first low rail and the gate. Penny now had five jumps—the low rail, the fence, the gate, the barrels, and the brush—more than enough for a good practice.

She was a little nervous as she took Bones through the first time. He was warmed up and anxious to go, but Penny knew they both had to be on their toes. She set off toward the first low rail. As they went over the rail, Penny's eyes were already on the next jump. They cleared that easily, too. Penny looked ahead to the gate. She remembered too well that she'd fallen at the obstacle before. She measured Bones's stride, collected him, squeezed with her legs, and over they went.

Now they were facing two jumps that were completely new to Bones. He'd have to make a longer jump over the barrels. Their takeoff was fine, but as Bones landed, his back hooves grazed the barrels, throwing him off-stride. Penny tried to collect him and pull him straight, but he was confused and made a mess of the brush jump. He jumped through it, rather than over it. Luckily, no harm was done. The brush just scattered out of the way, but Bones was snorting unhappily.

Mr. Billlings was already rebuilding the jump. "Don't worry," he said. "He's just got to get used to it."

Penny decided to concentrate on just the last two jumps. They moved the poles and the gate to the side, and Penny headed Bones directly toward the barrels. He remembered his nicked hooves and jumped almost too wide, but he went over the brush this time, not through it. Penny took him over again and again, and by the time she left for home, Bones could do the whole course without any mistakes.

Mr. Billings was smiling as she said good night. "Keep up the good work, Missy. See you tomorrow."

Seven

School was out! Penny jumped off the school bus and called to the other kids, "See you in the fall! Have a good summer!" Penny certainly would. She couldn't wait!

That night at the dinner table she showed her parents her report card. She'd made the honor roll again, just as she'd promised.

"Very good!" her mother said. "Although I see your math grade dropped from a B+ to a B."

Penny wrinkled her nose. "You know math isn't my favorite subject."

"Well, we can't complain about a B." Her father smiled at her. "Guess all this time with the horse hasn't taken as much time away from your studies as we thought."

Penny sighed with satisfaction. That was one hurdle behind her. Now she could *really* concentrate on Bones!

Penny decided it was time to go and watch one of Jan's riding lessons. It was fine to practice alone with Bones, but she needed to see what kind of competition they'd be up against.

"You should get a good look at the ring and the jumps," Jan agreed, "and see how our instructor explains things."

On the day of Jan's next lesson, Jan's mother drove both girls to the stable.

"I hear that you're doing very well with your riding," Mrs. Gilman said. "You must be pretty determined to try to do it all by yourself."

"Oh, I am. Of course, Jan's really been helping me."

"I'm looking forward to this show at the end of summer. I'll have two winners to cheer on."

"We hope!" Jan and Penny giggled.

Penny absolutely loved the stables. She felt at home among the smells of horses, hay, and leather. She loved all the excitement and chatter among the riders as she walked through the barns and talked to the various horses. She wondered how Bones would like it here. She could almost imagine him standing in one of the boxes. He'd probably enjoy the company of other horses, but she wondered if he might miss all his freedom in the pasture.

The riders in the class brought their horses out to the front of the barn and tied them to a long rail. Penny watched them as they tacked up. There were five riders in Jan's group—one boy and four girls. They'd all been riding for years and seemed to take it so for granted.

"Do you ride?" a girl named Mary Lou asked Penny. Mary Lou was slim, pretty, and perfectly dressed.

"Yes . . . well, I'm learning. I'm teaching an old horse to jump."

Mary Lou didn't seem very impressed. "You ought to take lessons here. This is the best stable around—best horses, best teachers." Her tone implied that it was the "only" place to ride.

Penny only nodded. She felt out of her depth as Mary Lou turned to the young rider at her side and started talking about the Ridgewood show and the new jacket and boots she'd gotten.

"Two hundred dollars for the boots," Mary Lou said, "but you can't find decent ones for less."

Penny looked away. She'd thought she was lucky to be able to borrow a pair of Jan's old boots. Well, she and Bones would show them that you didn't need a pair of two-hundred-dollar boots to ride well!

When the class entered the outside ring, Penny took a seat on the wooden bleachers at the far side. The ring was large—almost the size of Bones's pasture. Jan waved to Penny as she rode in on the big white mare that was her regular mount. The instructor, a young woman in her twenties, strode out to the center of the ring. She called to the riders. "Okay, start warming them up."

The riders immediately started off at a walk around the outside of the ring. Penny watched them with analytical eyes as they trotted, then cantered, then went on to figure eights. She studied every rider's seat and hands and the way the horses responded. Jan looked good, but to Penny's disappointment, so did the girl with the two-hundred-dollar boots.

The class progressed to warm-up jumps—a crossbar, some low rails, and a combination jump. Penny studied the last. She and Bones would need something like that. It looked fairly easy to set up. Two low fences a stride apart, then a higher and wider one. She watched Jan go through—lift, land, lift, land, lift, land. Penny realized she was unconsciously moving her upper body and squeezing with her legs as if she were in the saddle. She grinned to herself.

The instructor started pointing out a course to the class. Jumps of varying sizes and shapes had been set up all over the ring. Penny saw that the members of the class were to jump the fences down one side of the ring, then come around and up through the center. They would take two fences there, circle back down the other side, cut across the ring, and finish with the wall. Penny's eyes widened at the size of this last obstacle—at least four feet high and two feet wide. It was painted to look like a stone wall, but was constructed out of plywood. Nearly every one of the jumps on the intended course was much more difficult than anything Penny and Bones had attemped. She felt discouraged, but put her worries aside as the first rider, the boy, started out.

She didn't envy him being first. He started out fine and took the first three jumps without any problems, but as he circled to come up the center, Penny knew before the instructor spoke that he'd taken the turn too wide. He was at an angle approaching the next fence.

"Pull him up," the instructor yelled. "Do that fence again."

He slowed his horse, turned him, and approached again. Penny could see he was nervous. His horse sensed it. The horse knocked off the pole at the next jump and refused the one after. The instructor made him try twice more. Finally he got over and went on to finish the course, but without much style. He looked shaky. Jan gave him a sympathetic look, but Penny noticed that Mary Lou smiled snidely. Penny couldn't help but hope that the girl would take a fall.

No such luck. Mary Lou went through the course with perfection, and she knew it. Jan did almost as well. The instructor only called out to her once. "Heels down! Now *squeeze* over that last fence."

After everyone had done the course, the instructor started moving some fences around and raising bars. She even placed a bar above the wall. Penny's eyes widened. She swallowed hard when she heard the instructor's next words.

"If any of you intend to enter the big show, then you'd better be able to handle this course. It's not exactly what you'll face in the show, but the difficulty's about the same. Who's first?"

Penny noticed the boy didn't volunteer. One of the other girls didn't look too eager, either. Both of them were experienced riders. If they were hesitant, how would she and Bones fare?

Finally the instructor motioned to Jan to go out first. Penny crossed her fingers for her friend. Jan's expression was serious as she started the mare forward, cantered her in a circle, then approached the first fence.

"Whew!" Penny sighed as Jan got over cleanly. Penny noticed how Jan kept her eyes up, always looking forward and turning her head in the direction of the next fence.

Jan had completed half the course when she lost a stirrup coming over the brush. She held her leg tight against the mare's side as they approached the oxer, which had two top rails with a spread of about a foot between them. The takeoff was okay, but as they landed Jan lost her balance and fell. Penny jumped to her feet, but Jan seemed okay. In a moment Jan stood up. Her right hand still gripped the reins, but her left hand rubbed the small of her back.

The instructor came over. "Good try, but if you'd grabbed her mane when you came over, that wouldn't have happened. Start her again at the oxer."

As Jan remounted, she looked toward the bleachers. Penny mouthed the words, "You can do it."

Jan finished off the course with only a couple of ticks on the top rail. The other kids smiled at her—except for "Miss Boots."

Miss Boots went last, but maybe she'd planned it that way. She had a clean round, and her nose was up in the air when she finished.

"Yuk," Penny said to herself.

"That's it for today," the instructor called. "Cool them out." She left the ring as everyone dismounted. Penny went over to join Jan as she started walking the mare.

"You looked great, Jan."

"I could have been better." Jan sounded tired. "Mary Lou certainly showed us how to do it. Of course, that's her own horse, and her father paid a bundle for him."

Penny made a face. "What a snob. I've been calling her Miss Boots, since she was bragging about how much her new ones cost."

"Sounds like her." Jan frowned. "Too bad she's such a good rider."

"I think you're just as good."

"Maybe, but I'm not riding the same quality horse. The mare tries hard . . . don't you, babe," she said as she patted the mare's neck. "But she can't keep up with Mary Lou's horse, Dino."

"You shouldn't have to compete in the show against someone who owns her own horse," Penny protested.

"I won't have to," Jan answered. "There are different classes—ones for rider-owned horses and others for stable-owned."

"Then I'd never have to compete against her either." Penny was almost disappointed. Wouldn't she just love to show Miss Boots up! Then again, she had a long way to go.

"I don't know how they'd classify Bones," Jan said. "You don't own him, but he's not a stable horse either. I'll have to check."

Penny kicked at the dust with her toe. "I don't think I'm going to be good enough—or Bones either—by the end of the summer."

"Why not? Oh, you're thinking you'll have to go over a course like that?" Jan smiled. "You won't. There are different levels of jump classes. You and Bones could enter the intermediate."

Penny relaxed, but she was still feeling a lot less confident than she'd felt before watching the lesson. The kids in the class were so good. She and Bones still had a lot to learn.

She went back to work with a frenzy. The long summer days stretched on, and Penny spent nearly dawn to dusk with the horse.

By the middle of July, she'd saved enough money from baby-sitting to have Bones shod. Mr. Billings had given her the phone number of a farrier, a man trained to look after horses' feet, who had been out to trim Bones's hooves when they grew too long. She and Jan had both been checking the condition of Bones's hooves. He looked sound, but shoes were a wise idea with all the extra work he was doing. With the summer heat, the pasture ground was growing harder, too.

Penny and Mr. Billings were waiting the morning the farrier arrived. They watched with interest as he removed his tools and portable anvil from the back of his truck.

"Do you think Bones will behave himself?" Penny asked Mr. Billings.

"He's been shod before, years ago. Behaved himself then."

The farrier knew what he was doing. He talked in a firm but soothing voice to Bones as he worked on each hoof, trimming, filing, measuring, and fitting the shoes. He shaped them on his portable anvil, then nailed them in place. Since the outside wall of a horse's hoof is much like a human fingernail, Bones felt no pain. Soon he was clopping much more noisily across the gravel drive and back to his pasture.

Eight

"Morning, stranger," Penny's brother greeted her over the breakfast table the next day. Their parents had already finished and left the room.

"Why do you say that?" Penny peered around the cereal box.

"Well, we never see you around here anymore. You might as well be from another planet."

"I've been busy with Bones, Jimmy, you know that."

"Yeah. Must be some super horse to keep you that interested."

"Why don't you come and watch? Jan'll be there. We're practicing some bigger jumps today."

"Can I?" Her brother perked up, then he remembered himself. " 'Course that means I'll have to give up a day's fishing. Found a great new spot."

Penny made a face at him, picked up her cereal bowl, and took it to the sink. "If you're coming, get ready. I'm leaving in a minute."

Jimmy was after her like a shot.

When they arrived at the pasture, he stood safely outside the fence as she called Bones and started to groom him.

"He sure is big," Jimmy remarked.

"About average for a horse. Why don't you give him a carrot? He won't bite—just hold it out on the palm of your hand."

Jimmy looked a little nervous as he stiffly held the treat under Bones's muzzle. The horse lipped it up. Jimmy immediately withdrew his hand. Bones stepped closer to the fence.

"See?" Penny smiled. "He wants to be your friend."

Jimmy eyed the horse warily. "I'd rather have a new dirt bike."

Jan arrived then, and soon Mr. Billings appeared as well. Penny introduced her brother.

"You taking up riding, too?" Mr. Billings asked the boy.

"N-o-o," Jimmy answered. "I don't think so."

"That makes two of us, then," the old man said, chuckling. "Figure I'd rather have my bones all in one piece. You can sit with me over here on the fence and watch."

Soon the day's lesson was underway. Jan and Penny had set up jumps all over the pasture, trying to duplicate what Penny would encounter at a show. They started warming up over a combination jump. Then they went on to do half the course. Their plan was to work up gradually to jumping the whole course.

Bones was in high spirits, showing off for his enlarged audience. Penny had to keep him firmly collected as she took him over the fences down the length of the pasture, turned him for the brush, then turned him again to end the series with the gate.

She had to carefully judge his stride, and the fences were higher today. Everything felt exactly right as she urged him toward the gate and squeezed. Over they flew, perfectly. Penny was

65

justly pleased with their performance. She relaxed in the saddle and started to ease Bones back to a trot.

Suddenly Bones leaped forward as if he'd been stung. Penny didn't know what had happened. She tried to pull her wits together. Bones was pounding away with her, straight toward the oxer. She couldn't stop him! He surged over the oxer without any urging with an incredible leap that almost bounced her out of the saddle. She reached for his mane and clung for dear life as she tried to bring him back under control. He was heading straight for the pasture fence. She had a horrible vision of him trying to jump it, and the two of them ending in disaster on the other side. Penny was frozen in panic.

At the very edge of the fence, Bones skidded to a stop. In pure reaction, Penny slid from the saddle to her feet and stood at his head holding onto the reins. She was shaking like a leaf.

She barely noticed Jan running toward her. "Awesome!" Jan cried. "That was some jump!"

In a daze, Penny stared at her friend. Why did Jan sound happy? Penny could have broken her neck! She noticed with amazement that Mr. Billings and Jimmy were grinning from ear to ear, too. What was the matter with all of them?

Jan had reached Penny's side. She didn't seem to know who to hug first—Penny or Bones. "This guy is unbelievable! A good two feet to spare! How'd you do it?"

Penny's knees felt like water. "Do it? What do you mean? He took off with me!"

Jan frowned. "You didn't try to jump the oxer?"

"No. I was pulling him up. Then he just ran off like a shot."

"Must have been the backfire." Jimmy's eyes were nearly popping as he leaned against the rail. "It probably scared him."

"What backfire?"

"Just before you jumped the last time. Didn't you hear it?"

Penny shook her head.

"Well, old Bones here sure must have." Mr. Billings chuckled.

"Everyone seems to think it's so funny!" Penny growled. "Do you know how scared I was? I thought he was going to jump right out of the pasture."

"Yeah, I bet that was scary," Jan put in quickly. "But none of us guessed you were in trouble. The thing is, Penny, that this horse can *jump*! He just cleared six feet. Unbelievable!" she said again.

Penny stared at Bones. True, she'd felt like she was flying, but she'd thought it was because she was unprepared. "Six feet?" she said weakly.

Jan nodded.

"But he did it because he was scared," Penny said.

"If he can do it once, he can do it again. With the right training, he has the makings of a *first-class* jumper."

"Bones?" Penny said incredulously.

Mr. Billings was skeptical, too. "My old nag? Don't those classy jumpers have to be Thoroughbreds? Just look at him."

"Looks haven't got anything to do with it," Jan said. "He's got the hindquarters and the heart. That's what's important."

"Hmmmm." Mr. Billings considered this. "Well, Missy, he's got plenty of heart, that's for sure."

"We're going to have to start raising some of these jumps." Jan was already studying the course and planning.

Bones's achievement was slowly sinking into Penny's muddled brain. This was more than she'd dreamed. But if Bones was as good as Jan claimed, would Penny be able to ride him with the necessary expertise? She gazed at the old horse and shook her head. "You're full of surprises, aren't you, old boy? But next time, give me some warning!"

In a few minutes Penny had stopped shaking. Jan insisted they go right back to work. To get Bones used to jumping higher, they set up a gymnastic—a five-fence combination, with each fence slightly higher than the previous one. The fences were spaced so that Bones would land, gather, and immediately lift for the next jump.

Jan stood alongside the jumps as Penny put Bones through. "Squeeze!" Jan yelled each time Bones landed between fences.

Penny closed her legs on Bones's sides. They lifted again. The procedure was repeated up until the last fence, where Bones unexpectedly balked.

"You didn't prepare him," Jan called. "You didn't keep up the rhythm. Do it again!"

They practiced until Penny felt she would drop right out of the saddle. Bones had worked up a sweat, too. After she'd untacked him, Penny sponged him down and worked a sweat scraper over his coat to pull out the extra moisture. Then she walked him for thirty minutes to cool him out.

While she worked, the others jabbered excitedly about Bones's unexpected jumping ability. Penny listened and smiled—six feet! When Bones felt cool and dry to her touch, Penny measured out his grain and brought the bucket to the pasture. She was tempted to give him an extra ration as a reward, but too much grain could cause stomach troubles for the horse. And colic could be deadly.

Bones dug into his food. Mr. Billings brought out a bag of cookies and some sodas for the rest of them. Penny suddenly realized that she was starved. She grabbed a handful of cookies and plopped down on the grass. She was exhausted and knew her muscles would be sore later on—but what a day!

At home Penny made a valiant effort to hide her aching muscles, but her mother had noticed her frequent morning stiffness.

"There's a heating pad in the linen closet," her mother suggested with a smile a few mornings later. "You might want to use it tonight when you go to bed."

"Thanks, Mom," Penny said in surprise. "I would."

"Jimmy was pretty impressed with your riding the other day," her mother added.

"He told you?"

"Mmmm. Don't be surprised if he's up there watching you every afternoon."

"Why don't you come up?" Penny asked.

"We'll see, if I have time." Her mother paused. "Jimmy said that you're entering a show at the end of summer."

"Yes, that's what we're training for. And we'll win, too!"

"Penny, are you sure that's a good idea? You'd be competing against people who've had professional training. You've just started riding. I don't want to see you disappointed."

"I won't be."

Her mother didn't look very convinced. "I hope not. I'm afraid you're expecting too much of yourself and that horse."

That afternoon Penny was taking Bones over the double fence with the rails brought up to five feet. When he refused at the last moment, she went flying over his head and landed on her own.

Penny was completely stunned by the fall. She lay sprawled on the grass where she'd landed until Mr. Billings came running over.

Mr. Billings knelt at her side. "You okay, Missy? No, no, don't move! You might have broken something."

Penny didn't feel any sharp pains; she only felt terribly dizzy. "I'm okay . . . I think," she mumbled. She tried to sit up, and Mr. Billings helped support her. She rubbed her hand over her forehead.

"That was some tumble," the old man said. His voice was rough, and he cleared his throat quickly.

"My fault," Penny whispered. She'd allowed her concentration to slip and had brought Bones in too close.

"Don't worry about that now. Just sit still for a minute."

But Penny was made of sterner stuff than that. She pulled her legs under her and cautiously stood up, thankful for Mr. Billings's helping hands. Her legs felt shaky.

Bones had walked around the fence to join them. He was nickering anxiously. Penny reached out and laid her hand on his nose.

"It's okay, boy. Not your fault."

The horse still hung his head.

"Come on," Mr. Billings said gruffly. "I'm going to help you over to the side of the pasture and sit you down for a while. Don't worry about Bones. I'll get him unsaddled and take care of his feed."

Penny nodded. She knew she should never end a practice with a bad jump, but she didn't feel steady enough to get back in the saddle.

She leaned back on the pasture fence post in the cool shade of a nearby maple. Her head slowly began to clear. What was wrong with her? All day long she'd been making mistakes. She'd been bringing Bones up on the wrong lead, misjudging his stride. They were getting close to the show, and every workout was so important now. Yet she hadn't been able to concentrate. She'd been thinking about her mother's words that morning. She'd been wondering if her mother was right, if she had taken on too big a challenge.

Mr. Billings had removed Bones's saddle and bridle. He walked him over to the fence and tied his halter rope to the rail. He studied Penny. "Your color's coming back. Those freckles don't look like

71

they've been painted on your face anymore." He wagged his head. "Had me worried, you did."

"I feel better now, Mr. Billings."

"Just let me get him settled, and you come in the house and have some cookies and milk."

"Okay," Penny agreed, though she didn't feel very hungry. She felt discouraged and confused and a little angry with herself.

She didn't begin to feel better until she talked to Jan that night on the phone. Penny hadn't told her parents about the fall, and fortunately Jimmy hadn't been there to see it.

"Everybody takes a bad fall once in a while," Jan told her. "You shouldn't feel so bummed, Penny. You and Bones are doing terrific. The way you're going, the two of you will be good enough for the advanced jumping class."

Penny wanted to believe that, but her self-confidence had taken a blow. "Will you come over to Mr. Billings's tomorrow? I think I need some more coaching."

"Sure. I'll be there."

Nine

Penny didn't feel her usual confidence as she got into the saddle the next day. Still, the workout went well. Jan's coaching helped a lot. At least Penny was sure of what she was doing right and wrong.

"What I think you need to do," Jan told her later, "is to bring Bones up to the stable and try him over the fences there."

"Would they mind?"

"I'll talk to the stable manager. I don't think he would. He might charge you what he would for a lesson, and we'll have to arrange to go up when there aren't any lessons going on."

"I can afford the price of one lesson, I suppose," Penny said, considering. "Practicing there would do us both good. We're only guessing now what fences we'll have to face."

"Well, the ring won't be set up the same as for the show. They move the fences around all the time, but you can get a feel for it."

Penny nodded and twirled a strand of hair around her finger. "You know, Jan, I don't know why I got so nervous after that fall. I trust Bones. I trust myself, really. I only wish my mother and father believed in us, too. I can tell they still don't think my riding's important."

"Wait till they see you in the show. They're coming, aren't they?"

"They'd better. I'll make sure they *promise!*"

"I'm going to pick up the entry forms this week. The manager said you should ride in the rider-owned class. Remember, you're going to have to pay a twenty-five-dollar entry fee."

Penny nodded. She'd already set aside enough baby-sitting money. Of course, with all her expenses for Bones, she had nothing left for herself, but that was okay. "I can still borrow your old riding outfit, can't I?"

"*Of course* you can. There are a couple of grass stains on the breeches, but we can get them out. I'll ask my mother what to use."

Penny was still thinking ahead. "I'll have to ride Bones over to the stable, but that shouldn't be any problem. Now that he's got shoes, the pavement won't bother him."

"Let me check with the manager tomorrow when I have my lesson," Jan offered. "You should take him up to the stable as soon as you can. Only three and a half weeks till the show!"

Jan phoned Penny the next night. "I've got it all set. You can bring Bones up tomorrow. Terry Mullins—the manager—didn't mind since you're going to be riding in the show. He said to come up at two, in between afternoon classes. They always give the stable horses an hour's break."

"Okay," Penny agreed, "but tomorrow is so *soon!*" She wrapped the phone cord around her fingers. "Boy, this makes me kind of nervous. Bones isn't used to a lot of people and horses around."

"He's going to have to get used to it. The bleachers will be full on show day."

"I guess. . . ."

Penny had a hard time sleeping that night. In her mind she took herself and Bones through everything they'd done so far. When she finally fell asleep, her dreams were filled with images of jumping and stumbling and knocking down poles.

She woke up feeling like she hadn't slept at all. She took a shower, got dressed, and, with Jimmy tagging along, was at Mr. Billings's by nine-thirty.

Penny was glad Jimmy had decided to come. His rambling, never-ending talk kept her from thinking about her dreams. She groomed and saddled Bones. The horse seemed full of life and ready to conquer the world that morning. As she mounted, Jimmy shouted out encouraging words— at least words he thought were encouraging.

"Rev him up, Sis!" He made some engine noises for accompaniment. "Now, if I was in a racing car or on a dirt bike—"

"Never mind!" Jumping a horse required altogether different skills, Penny thought.

She put Jimmy's comments and her dreams out of her mind as she warmed up Bones. Jan had said to practice turns and unexpected fences. Without moving any fences, there were several opportunities among the fences they'd set up. She could almost jump a serpentine.

Penny started Bones off. This was where her ability as a rider was so important. It was up to her to look ahead to the next obstacle and prepare him. She started him around the lower end of the pasture, where she took him over the rail and the low brush. She turned him and headed him across toward the barrels. He jumped and cleared, but he seemed confused. This wasn't the course he usually followed.

Penny gathered the reins and turned him again, keeping tight pressure on her inside leg so that he bent his body around it. She headed him toward the low gate. Bones jumped and cleared it easily, even though they were approaching it from the opposite direction. She turned him again in an "S" and headed toward the combination at the top of the pasture.

He loved the combination and surged over the four fences. Penny turned him again toward the wall. He hesitated for a moment, then understood, and cantered ahead. She barely had to measure his stride as he approached and soared over.

Penny circled him down to a slower pace and smiled to herself. She didn't have to doubt herself anymore. She could get Bones through the unexpected—in style!

"Good boy!" She rubbed her hand up and down his neck. His ears flicked back. "That's the way!"

He seemed to appreciate her compliments and pranced sideways.

"Hey, Sis," Jimmy called from the rail. "Not bad! My money's on you in the show."

"Oh, Jimmy! You watch too much TV."

Penny carefully groomed Bones before leaving for the stables. She wanted him to look good next to all the stable horses. She also groomed herself and put on her borrowed habit and boots. She hadn't had time to wash the breeches, so a couple of grass stains showed, but they weren't as noticeable as Jan had thought.

Both Bones and Penny looked their best as Penny rode up Mr. Billings's drive. He'd come out to see them off.

"Be careful of the cars," he said worriedly. "He's not used to it anymore. Ride up off the pavement."

"Don't worry, Mr. Billings, we'll be fine." Penny had every intention of being careful. "Bones means too much to me. I'd never take a chance with him."

The old man smiled. "Right. I know that. Just an old man's worries. But bet your life I'll be up at that stable for the show."

Penny grinned. "You'd better be."

Mr. Billings waved her off, and Penny headed Bones out to the road for their mile-and-a-half ride.

They didn't meet too much traffic. Bones did look nervously sideways every time a car passed. There were no sidewalks and there was plenty of room to walk along the side, but some of the roads were narrow and winding, so Penny kept a tight rein on the horse.

They arrived at the stable without mishap. As they walked up the drive into the stable yard, Bones's ears shot forward when he heard whinnies from the barn. Bones answered them loudly and excitedly. He hadn't been around another horse for a while. He fought the pressure on his reins and tried to go in the direction of the barn. Penny rode him as far as the bar where the riders tacked up and dismounted.

A few horses popped their heads over the open stall half-doors along the outside of the barn. Bones snorted, whinnied, pranced, and tried to get closer. Penny saw that she was going to have trouble getting him to concentrate on jumping.

She took him along the outside line of the stables and walked him from stall to stall. It was a long process. Bones stopped to touch noses, sniff, and check each of the stall occupants. They nickered back and forth in their own language. Some of the stall dwellers turned away at Bones's curiosity. Others tried to be quite friendly.

When Penny finally pulled Bones away, he came reluctantly and in obvious rebellion.

Jan met her back in front of the stable. "I kind of figured that would happen," she said. "He hasn't been around other horses."

"Yeah, but is he going to be able to concentrate on the jumping?"

"Maybe he'll snap out of it once he sees the jumps," Jan said hopefully.

Several curious riders and stable hands had stepped outside to see what the commotion was about. Bones pricked his ears as he studied these new people. He sidestepped nervously. Penny tried to soothe him. "Easy, easy, boy," she whispered.

"Get out there," Jan said under her breath, "before he gets any more nervous. You've only got forty-five minutes."

Penny agreed uncertainly. From the way Bones was acting, she didn't have very high hopes for their performance. She quickly led Bones away before any of the curious onlookers had a chance to ask questions. She opened the gate to the ring, led Bones through, and secured the latch again. This was all so new to her. She felt uneasy, and Bones wasn't helping. He looked back at the stable block and took no interest in the course. Penny mounted and started walking him around the ring.

She was conscious of every movement she made. All those eyes watching. She refused to turn around and look, but when she and Bones came up the other side of the ring, she saw the small crowd gathered outside the stable.

Concentrate, concentrate, she told herself. Forget them. She only wished that Bones would forget them. She took him through a couple of figure eights at a trot and canter. By then Jan had come to join them and stood at the rail.

The sound of her voice was soothing to Penny.

"Take him down along the outside for starters," Jan said quietly. "Just those three fences."

Penny nodded, turned Bones, and put him into a canter. She circled toward the first fence. She tried her best, but Bones was not paying attention. He looked everywhere but where he should.

"Come on, Bones," Penny whispered in his ear. "Forget them. Relax. Jump . . . that's what you like to do."

His ears flicked. He'd heard her voice. Feeling more assured, Penny put him to the first fence. He didn't give his normal, strong leap. He practically climbed over the fence. Penny gritted her teeth. If he wasn't going to concentrate, then she must concentrate doubly to make up for it. She gently pulled on his reins to wake him up, headed him toward the next fence, and squeezed hard. He went over, but without any style. He was behaving like a plodding old workhorse.

"Darn you, Bones!" Penny cried. "Don't be dumb. Jump! You can show them."

They finished the first three fences sloppily. Bones didn't seem to care. His mind was on the horses in the stable and on the people watching. Several of the waiting riders had come to stand beside the ring fence. They were laughing.

Penny's cheeks were red with humiliation as she rode Bones through the combination. He cleared all the fences, but no better than the worst school pony.

"She's going to ride him in the show?" one of the spectators called to Jan. "Ought to be good for the booby prize."

Another voice rang out. "Mr. Mullins is crazy to allow an entry like that. Thought you said they were so good! They're not ready for the beginner class."

Penny saw that Mary Lou was among the observers. She was smiling condescendingly. "She's training an old horse to jump," she said, "and doesn't know how herself. Can you imagine?" A jeering chorus of laughter followed. It was hushed when the stable manager walked over.

Penny was red to the roots of her hair. She felt like sinking into her riding habit and disappearing. She wanted to cry, but she knew she and Bones could do it—if only he'd pay attention!

In frustration, she decided to do something she'd never done before. She rode over to Jan, who was standing on the rail away from the rest of the crowd. Jan looked pretty embarrassed herself.

"I told them," Jan mumbled, "that Bones was National Horse Show quality."

"You didn't!" Penny cried.

Jan looked pathetic. "Well, they were making jokes—"

"Never mind." Penny again gritted her teeth. "Give me a crop."

"Crop? You never use a crop."

"Give me one—please."

Jan reached behind her, where several crops were resting on the bottom seat of the bleachers in case the riding school needed them. Penny took one.

"He may not like it," Jan said.

"But he's going to wake up," Penny said with determination. "I won't use it unless I absolutely have to." She turned away from the rail. Subtly she tapped the end of the crop on Bones's shoulder. He danced sideways in surprise. She tucked the crop into the top of her boot. When Penny turned him, he looked toward the jumps with the first interest he'd shown.

But the giggles from the other side of the ring were upsetting him, too. His nostrils widened and quivered.

Penny leaned over the saddle. "Don't let them make jerks of us, Bones. You can show them, and so can I. But I can't do it alone, boy. You've got to help me. Jump like you've been doing. Come on. Get with it!"

Bones flicked his ears. He whoofed air through his nose, then suddenly he seemed to pull himself together.

Penny started cantering him. His tail was up this time, his ears forward. She was going for all or nothing. She wasn't afraid for Bones's ability. He'd done as much in their practice rounds at the pasture, and her own will to succeed was like an iron rod.

Penny was going to do the whole course. She set Bones toward the first fence.

He was still slightly distracted as he went over. He didn't wake up completely until Penny touched the crop to his shoulder again. She hadn't hurt him with it, but the touch was enough. She felt his muscles gather, to the point that she had to hold him back for the next jump.

He soared over, and now he was interested again. His hooves drummed beneath her, and Penny readied him for the next jump. They took it cleanly. Penny turned him to cut across the ring. Bones saw the next fence four strides ahead—a brush with a pole above. Penny steadied him. One, two, three, four, she counted, squeeze. They headed to the next fence, and a sharp turn within only four strides. She gathered him as they came around the turn and moved toward the combination.

Bones popped over as if the three- and four-foot rails didn't exist. As they went into the next tight corner, Penny looked ahead. Double brush, double poles, and the wall. She turned her head to direct her eyes over the first of the obstacles. Bones moved with her, his muscles bunching and relaxing as he cantered forward. Penny realized he was going too fast. She shortened his stride slightly, then pressed with her legs. Bones took the brush with a foot to spare, then the double rail. In front of them was the fence that had always daunted Penny—the wall, with a rail on top. Since it was both high *and* wide, Penny figured Bones would have to jump at least five and a half feet to clear it.

She accelerated Bones's canter, then collected him just before the jump and squeezed hard. The extra energy went into his jump. He soared.

Penny circled him and breathed a sigh of relief. They'd gotten through! She noticed some of the spectators had walked over toward Jan. She heard bits and pieces of conversation. "Not bad! He *can* jump." Then she heard Mary Lou's distinctive voice. "Don't believe it. They must have been lucky!"

Penny dismounted, rubbed Bones's nose, and gave him a piece of apple from her pocket. Jan came into the ring. She was grinning. "You did it."

"I finally got him to go," Penny sighed. "But I'm still worried about the show. If it takes as long for him to relax . . ."

"It won't. He's getting used to it."

"Did we look all right?" Penny said worriedly.

Jan beamed. "Are you kidding?"

They were interrupted as Terry Mullins, the manager of the stable, came over. There was a light of excitement in his eyes, but he only reached up to rub Bones's head.

"You're riding in the end-of-summer show, I hear."

"Yes," Penny nodded. She reached in her pocket and pulled out some bills. "Here's the money for today."

"Thanks. Where'd you find this horse?" He looked Bones over with appreciation.

Penny was surprised at his interest. "An old farmer friend of mine owns him. I asked him if I could take care of him and ride him in exchange."

"Who trained him?"

"Jan and I."

"No outside help?" He cast them a disbelieving look.

"Just us," Penny said seriously.

He widened his eyes but only said, "Which class are you entering?"

"Intermediate."

"Why not try the junior advanced?"

"Us?" Penny said. "It's our first show."

"Mmmm." He hesitated. "The horse had a bad start. He was nervous, but I saw you wake him up. He's got his heart in it." He looked at Penny. "Think about it."

"Y-yes, I will," Penny managed to mumble.

Mr. Mullins turned and went back to the stable building.

Penny stared at Jan. "I don't believe it!"

"Neither do I," Jan whispered. "Bones has the potential, but for his first show?"

"That's what I think. It's too soon. I'd be a nervous wreck. I'd never win."

"Taking a third or fourth would be good in *that* class."

But I want to be first, Penny thought.

Penny mounted and headed Bones down the stable drive. She could have stayed to watch Jan's lesson, but she wanted to be alone to think. Her head was spinning. So much had happened in the last hour. She was still amazed that the stable manager was so impressed with her and Bones. She felt so proud of what they had accomplished, but she realized how much more they had to do. Bones would have to get used to crowds, and Penny knew in her heart that it was too soon for them to think of the advanced class. But some day . . .

Ten

Penny and Jan filled out entry forms for the show the next day. Jan agreed with Penny's decision not to enter the advanced class. It *was* too soon. Penny checked off the Intermediate Hunters Over Fences category and gave Jan the entry fee. There were a dozen different classes to choose from, both jumping and equitation classes. Penny and Bones would have plenty of opportunities for future shows.

Penny broke their daily practice into two lessons—one each in the morning and afternoon. She and Bones had time to rest in between so they'd be fresh for each session.

Jan spent extra time coaching them. When Jan was there, they practiced the most difficult fences and maneuvers—tight turns and combinations of upright and spread jumps. Jan certainly let Penny know when she made a mistake.

"No, Penny! Collect him! It's only three strides to that jump. See, you've landed on the wrong lead. Pull him up! Fix his lead!"

Their friendship could easily have been hurt by Jan's sharp remarks, but Penny knew Jan was giving them valuable advice. Ignoring their mistakes wouldn't help them win the show. Instead Penny grew expert at lengthening and shortening Bones's stride and at judging when to do so.

"You'd think you were going out for the Olympics," her brother teased as he leaned over the pasture fence watching them.

"We have to practice twice as hard, Jimmy. We've only had a few months. The other kids have ridden for *years*."

"You'll beat them," he said confidently. "Mom and Dad said they're coming to the show," he added.

"I made them promise they would."

"I think they're worried you're not going to do very well."

Penny only smiled grimly. "I'll do okay."

Fortunately the summer had been a dry one. Penny's practice had only been interrupted by rain a few times. The rain turned the pasture to mud, but jumping in the mud was good experience, too. No one could know what the weather would be like on show day.

Penny's and Bones's muscles grew harder and firmer. They could practice for longer periods before tiring, and Penny no longer went home aching every night. They'd both be in top condition for the show.

"Terry Mullins was disappointed when he saw what class you'd entered," Jan told Penny a few afternoons later. "He looked through all the entries yesterday."

Penny wiped her damp brow and took off her hard hat. "But it wouldn't make sense for us to enter the junior advanced."

"I think he wants to wake up some people at the stable—'you-know-who' in particular. She's getting lazy and too cocky."

"Oh yeah?" Penny was all ears.

"She's not practicing hard enough. She thinks that she and Dino will walk away with the blue ribbon."

Penny smiled broadly, dimples showing. "Wouldn't it be funny if the competition got the jump on her? I'd love to see her face if she lost."

"Well, so far I haven't seen anyone good enough to do it—" Jan sighed, "—though there'll be other rider-owned entries. We won't know till the day of the show."

"Who's riding in my class?" Penny asked, almost afraid to hear the answer.

"Jeanie Collins—"

"She's in *your* lesson!"

"Yeah, but don't worry. She gets nervous at shows. There'll probably be some other kids who board horses at the stable, and entries from outside, but I haven't seen the final list. Don't worry. If Terry singled out you and Bones, he must think you've got a good chance."

Penny crossed out the days on her calendar as the show approached. One more week. She raised the poles on the jumps another notch. They were higher than what they'd face in the show, but it wouldn't hurt to have Bones expect the greater height. He'd clear the show fences with room to spare, she hoped.

She and Mr. Billings shifted some of the fences around, too. Bones had to be ready for an unfamiliar course. They wouldn't have an opportunity to practice over the show course. The riders would only be permitted to walk through the course and calculate distances between the fences right before the show.

Bones and Penny were really working like a team now. On the altered course, Bones was alert to her commands and immediately obeyed. There were a few times, too, when Penny misjudged a fence or a turn, and Bones saved them from an accident.

"He's a smart old nag, isn't he?" Mr. Billings remarked after he'd witnessed one of Bones's saving maneuvers. Penny had taken a corner too tight. Bones had seen he wouldn't have room for a decent takeoff. He'd scrambled sideways, gained an extra half-stride, and then approached the jump, clearing it at an angle.

"He's the best," Penny said, grinning. "I just hope I don't mess things up for us at the show."

"Just relax, Missy. You'll do fine."

Penny arrived early the next morning, eager to begin a full day of practice. She was surprised to find Mr. Billings out in the pasture with Bones. He was kneeling by Bones's right foreleg.

Penny ran over. "What's wrong?"

"Looked out the window this morning and saw him limping. Seems he got caught up on something during the night. Got quite a gash here just below his knee."

Penny was already squatting down to examine the wound, which was covered with dried blood. "Oh, no! What could he have done?"

"I found a rough railing at the far end of the pasture. There's a big clump of clover on the other side. He was probably trying to get at it and gashed his leg."

"What should I do, Mr. Billings?" Penny's face had gone pale. "Should I call a vet?"

"Naw. I've tended enough animals in my time. I've got some salve. We'll clean out the cut good and bandage it. Good thing he's had his tetanus shots. Going to have to keep him quiet for a few days, though, till it starts healing."

"The show's in five days!"

"Yup. This is a bad bit of luck. You hold him. I'll go fetch some soap and water and my salve."

"You poor baby," Penny crooned to Bones. She laid her head against his neck. "But we'll get you fixed up."

Mr. Billings returned with a basin of warm, soapy water, some towels, and an old piece of sheeting. "Here," he said to Penny, "you tear this sheet up in strips while I clean him up."

He worked gently with a damp cloth, washing away the dried blood and dirt. Bones snorted uneasily at the sting of the soap.

"Shhh. It'll be all right," Penny said in a soothing voice. She held his head until the cleaning was done.

Mr. Billings opened a can of salve and liberally smoothed it onto the wound. "Okay, give me that sheeting." Penny handed him a strip. He carefully wrapped it around Bones's lower leg, which would help keep the wound from getting dirty and possibly infected. He tied off the end. "Have to check this every day and keep it clean."

Penny nodded.

"Meanwhile, I think we ought to keep him in the stall. Less likely he'll open it up if he stays quiet." The old man rose and patted the horse. "I don't want to see anything go wrong. You've worked too hard."

"Do you think he'll be fit by Saturday?" Penny asked anxiously.

"Just have to wait and see, though I don't see why not. Funny, but last night after you left I was thinking that we should put him in the stall. I got it cleaned up and put down some bedding."

"Gee, I could have done that, Mr. Billings. You don't have to go to all that work."

"Wasn't any trouble." He seemed a little embarrassed. "Haven't had so much to interest me in a long time. Well, come on. Let's get him settled."

Penny was worried sick. Eventually Bones would be okay. The cut would heal, but would they be able to compete in the show? She stayed by Bones's stall, giving him all the attention she could. The next day she led him around the pasture at a walk. He had to have some exercise. Mr. Billings cleaned and rebandaged the leg.

"It's healing," he said. "No infection. Maybe tomorrow we can take the dressing off."

Jan came over, and they commiserated with each other. "What a shame!" Jan said. "I was getting so excited."

"He may still be okay for the show." Penny was trying to keep her hopes up.

"Yeah, I sure hope so. But that's five days without exercise or practice—for both of you."

"I've been doing my exercises at home."

"I hope his leg hasn't stiffened up. He may favor it, and it wouldn't be fair to try to jump him."

"I know," Penny murmured. "If he's stiff, I'll drop out of the show. I wouldn't do anything to hurt Bones." But if she dropped out of the show, she wouldn't be able to show her parents how well she was doing. When school started, she'd only be able to see Bones on the weekends.

Mr. Billings took off the dressing the next day. When Penny walked Bones, she didn't notice him favoring the leg at all, but at a faster pace, he might.

By Friday, the cut had healed further. Penny had a hard decision to make. Should she try to ride him, or forget the show? It wasn't a decision she felt she could make alone. She talked to Mr. Billings.

"He's your horse, Mr. Billings. I think you should decide."

The old man scratched his head. "Well, the cut's healing. Could open up, I suppose, but I'd hate like heck to have you lose everything now. Why don't you try him on a lead today at the faster paces. We'll see how he looks."

"Okay." Penny clipped the longe line to Bones's halter and brought him out to the pasture. Mr. Billings leaned on the fence to watch.

Bones didn't show any discomfort. His ears perked, and he seemed delighted to be outside. He'd obviously been bored in the stall. Penny walked him in a wide circle and studied his right foreleg. He was putting it down solidly.

"Now, trot him," Mr. Billings called.

She did. Bones eagerly picked up his pace. There was no sign of hesitation in his stride. He definitely wasn't favoring his injured leg. Penny trotted him over to Mr. Billings.

"Looks okay," the old man said. He ran his hands over the foreleg. "No infection."

"But he'll be doing a lot more stretching and pulling when he's jumping," Penny said honestly. "That might open the cut."

"Might and might not." Mr. Billings looked from Bones to Penny, then nodded to himself. "I think you should try the show."

"You're sure?" Penny felt her excitement building.

"Anything goes wrong with the leg, you just pull him out. And I'll be there tomorrow in case anything happens."

"Oh, thank you."

"Nothing to thank me for. Best you don't try any jumping till tomorrow, though. Give his leg another day."

Penny agreed wholeheartedly, but she knew the lack of practice would make it harder for both of them in the show.

"We'll try our best, Mr. Billings."

"I know you both can do it."

Eleven

Penny was up at the crack of dawn. The first thing she did was look out the window. There wasn't a cloud in the sky. That was one thing in their favor. She was too nervous to eat much breakfast, but she took a shower and washed her hair. As it dried, she went through her checklist again. Her borrowed habit was spotlessly clean and pressed. She'd shined her boots and her saddle until she could see her face in them. She'd brushed her velveteen hard hat. And she had ribbons to braid into Bones's mane and tail.

She carefully folded her breeches, jacket, white shirt, and stock and put them in a bag. She wouldn't change until she was ready to ride Bones to the stable. When her hair was dry, she made one long, tight braid and pinned it up at the back of her head. It wouldn't do to have flyaway ends sticking out from under her hard hat.

Her stomach was fluttering with nervous butterflies as she gathered her things together and went back out to the kitchen. Her parents and her brother were at the table eating breakfast.

"Well, I'm leaving for Mr. Billings's." Penny went over to the table.

"Good luck," her mother said. She kissed Penny's cheek. "You're *sure* about this show?"

Penny nodded.

Her father gave her a squeeze. "We'll be up in time to watch you. One o'clock, you said?"

"The class goes off then. You should probably come a little earlier."

"You can do it, Sis," Jimmy said cheerfully. "I told everybody you're going to win."

Penny grinned. "Thanks, Jimmy. I hope so."

Mr. Billings was already in the yard when Penny arrived. He had his coffee cup in hand. "You're here bright and early!"

"Well, I've got a lot to do, Mr. Billings. Bones has to have a real good grooming."

"The old boy seems fit and chipper this morning," he said. "Just went in to check him and give him his morning's feed. Set your bag down on the back porch, and I'll bring him out."

Bones did look full of life. He seemed to sense that something exciting was happening that day. Mr. Billings brought him to the rail. "Leg looks good," he said. "Maybe we ought to bandage it up for the show. Just in case."

"We could bandage both forelegs," Penny suggested. "People do that a lot for shows."

"Make him look more stylish, eh?" Mr. Billings chuckled.

Penny nodded. "Do you think it's okay to trot him around this morning?"

"Don't see why not. Loosen him up a bit. I'd say he wants a little exercise."

Penny took Bones's lead rope and started off. She walked and trotted him for twenty minutes and watched his right foreleg carefully.

Mr. Billings had been studying the horse's movements, too. "He's sound for the time being," he said, nodding. "I've got some things to do in the house. Give a yell if you need me."

Penny set to work. Bones preferred being outdoors, so Penny carried her grooming materials to the pasture. Bones's appearance would be as important as her own. Penny curried him, then went over his coat with a body brush, and then a soft towel, until he gleamed. Next she shampooed his mane and tail, dried them, and brushed them out. She collected her ribbons and sectioned off his mane. As she braided each section, she wove in a length of ribbon, then tucked up the braid into a loop and neatly tied it off. She'd decided to braid only half his tail. She drew up sections of hair from the side of his tail, creating a French braid along the top, and tied it off with a bit of ribbon.

Her next step was to clean Bones's hooves and apply hoof oil to the outside.

When she was finished, she stood back and inspected him. "You look gorgeous, Bones—if I do say so myself!"

The horse craned his neck around in self-inspection and nickered in agreement.

All she had left to do was apply the bandages, but she needed Mr. Billings's help. She ran to the house and got him.

"If that don't beat all!" He chuckled when he saw Bones. "Looks dandy, doesn't he? Hope it won't go to his head. Let me fix up the bandages." He wrapped the strips neatly around each foreleg.

"Time you got yourself cleaned up, too," he said to Penny. "It's nearly eleven."

Penny had almost forgotten about herself. She ran and fetched her bag of clothes and used Mr. Billings's bathroom to change. When she was dressed, she studied herself in front of the mirror. She adjusted her stock, the white scarf she'd tied at her neck, repinned her braid, and secured her hard hat. She grinned at her reflection. Not bad.

She went out to tack up Bones, but Mr. Billings had already taken care of that for her.

"You'll need to tighten the girth some more."

"Yeah, he always blows up his stomach." Once she was in the saddle, Penny lifted the left stirrup, reached down and pulled up the girth buckle another notch. She dropped the stirrup and inserted her foot. "We're all set, I think." She let out a nervous breath.

"You look good to me, Missy." Mr. Billings walked with them through the gate to the drive. He looked up and winked. "Well, good luck. I'll see you up there in a bit."

"You know how to get to the stable?" Penny asked.

"Ought to know my way around this neighborhood by now. Careful riding over."

Penny tried to swallow her nervousness as she set off. She probably should have eaten something. Her stomach was jumping around like crazy. But she couldn't let Bones sense her jumpiness. She tried to take her mind off the show and just concentrate on getting there. In a moment she began to relax.

When they got close to the stable, she felt her nervousness return. Cars were parked on both sides of the street. She carefully walked Bones around them and into the stable drive. Equitation classes were going on. The bleachers were full of spectators, and others stood along the end of the show ring. One side of the drive was lined with horse vans. Some vans contained occupants. Many more horses were being led up and down the grass verge, and others were being ridden in the warm-up ring near the barns. The air buzzed with conversation and the calls of horses.

Bones was dancing on his toes in excitement. Penny had trouble holding him at a quiet walk. His ears were going every which way. He turned his head from side to side and tried to look at everything at once.

Penny decided the safest thing to do was to dismount and lead him. As she walked the nervous horse forward, she searched through the crowd. Jan would probably be up at the stable building getting her mare ready. Penny eased Bones through the crowd. There were so many people! And they'd all be watching her and Bones in the show. Somehow she hadn't thought about that many staring eyes.

Penny heard someone call her name. She looked around and saw Jan waving from the end of the barn. "Come over here!" Jan called.

It wasn't quite as hectic away from the show ring. But Bones was just as excited and skittish because the barn, of course, was filled with horses.

"Whew!" Penny said when she reached Jan's side. "This is incredible."

"This show is always packed. I've been watching for you. Bring Bones inside the barn. Boy! He looks good."

"Thanks." Penny walked Bones into the wide central aisle of the large building. Box stalls stretched down the length of the barn on both sides. Jan had her mare in crossties and was in the midst of grooming her. Other horses were in crossties being groomed further down.

Penny hesitated just inside the door.

"Come on," Jan said, motioning to her. "How's his leg? I see you've got him bandaged."

"It seemed okay this morning. Mr. Billings told me to go ahead and try."

Bones was huffing at the mare and pulling to go over.

"The mare's easygoing," Jan said. "Let him come over." Jan returned to her grooming, and Penny let Bones approach the mare. The two animals touched noses and sniffed each other. Bones seemed more than a little pleased with his new acquaintance and was making noises somewhere between a snort and a whinny.

"If he gets used to being around the other horses before your class, it should calm him down," Jan explained.

"I hope so," Penny sighed. "He was practically quivering when we came down the drive. I should check in and get my number. I've only got an hour till my class."

"Yeah, you should. The registration desk is in the stable office. You can leave Bones here. Clip him into the next set of crossties."

Jan seemed so calm. Penny wished she could be as relaxed. She brought the reins back over Bones's head, loosened his girth, backed him up, and attached the crossties. He wasn't happy about leaving the mare, but there were plenty of other horses to keep his thoughts occupied.

Penny walked around to the stable office, waited in line with other immaculately groomed riders, and gave her name and class to the lady at the desk. She took the cardboard square with her number—twelve—and was told what time to appear for her event. Penny tied her number across her back and wondered about the other riders. Most of them seemed as relaxed as Jan. They'd probably ridden in dozens of shows. Would she be competing against any of them? The thought didn't reassure her.

"Aren't you nervous at all?" she asked Jan when she returned to the barn.

"Are you kidding? I'm a wreck."

"But you don't act like it."

"You don't look nervous either."

Both girls laughed, and Penny felt better. It was nice to know she wasn't the only one with shaking knees. "What time is your class?" Penny asked.

"Right after yours." Jan was finished with the grooming and began tacking up the mare. "I've got to get dressed. Why don't you take Bones outside and meet me at the warm-up ring in a few minutes?"

Penny almost hated to return to the crowds and confusion. She saw that the equitation classes had finished up, and the judges were awarding ribbons. She looked around for her parents and Mr. Billings, but didn't see them. She only recognized a few faces from her previous visits to the stable. Mary Lou's was one of them. Miss Boots was standing outside the office with three other riders. All of them were dressed in expensive new outfits. Mary Lou, as usual, was laughing and looking super confident.

Penny turned away, and refused to look down at her own secondhand habit. Maybe some wonderful rider would appear to knock the wind out of Mary Lou's sails. There certainly were some beautiful horses at the show—very expensive horses. She'd noticed the riders of some of those expensive horses looking questioningly at Bones. Well, maybe Bones didn't look like a Thoroughbred, but she was proud of him. His beauty went below the surface.

Penny waited by the warm-up ring. She still hadn't seen her parents, and she was beginning to wonder if they'd come.

The equitation ribbons had been awarded. Workers were now scurrying around the show ring, setting up jumps that had been brought in on a flatbed trailer. Penny watched them. Other jumping classes would be called before hers—all the pony classes, and the stable-owned intermediate class. The course would probably be changed.

Jan walked up beside her. "Let's warm them up," she said. "I'll feel less jittery if I'm doing something."

Bones and the mare were touching noses again. The girls led them into the ring. They mounted and tightened their girths. A half-dozen riders were already warming up around the oval ring, and Bones immediately became distracted. He didn't like being behind the other horses and kept trying to increase his pace. Jan drew her mare alongside, and that seemed to quiet him. Gradually he started paying more attention to Penny's commands.

"He seems to be moving all right," Jan told Penny.

"But I haven't had him above a trot, and we haven't jumped in five days."

"You won't be the first out. Watch how the riders ahead of you do and see where they have problems. Then concentrate. Don't let anything distract you when you're in the ring."

"I just hope Bones can concentrate."

"He's getting better. He's not so excited."

Penny nodded. The time spent among the other horses had helped. He was getting used to the commotion. Now Penny only had to worry about his leg and the fact that they hadn't practiced recently. "Let me try him alone and see how he does," she said. Penny moved ahead of Jan along the rail and put Bones into a canter. He strode ahead without faltering, leading with his injured leg. Penny let him go around the ring three times, then pulled him back into a trot. His leg seemed fine.

The pony jumping classes had begun. Penny watched out of the corner of her eye as a petite little girl urged her Shetland around to a hand of applause. When Penny looked up, she saw Mr. Billings outside the warm-up ring. She rode Bones over to the gate, dismounted, and led him out.

"Some crowd," Mr. Billings said. "How's he doing?"

"He's quieting down. So far, so good."

"Let's have a look at that leg." Mr. Billings knelt down and checked the bandage. "It'd be bleeding through if he'd opened that cut. No sign of blood."

Penny heard a taunting voice somewhere behind them—Mary Lou's.

"Will you look at her making a fuss over that old horse. You'd think he was a champion! They haven't got a chance—even in intermediate."

Penny's eyes flashed.

Mr. Billings laid a calming hand on her arm. "Someone you know?"

"Oh, just some stuck-up girl."

"Pay her no mind. Doesn't know what she's talking about."

But Mary Lou's words had put steel in Penny's spine. She forgot most of her nervousness and became more determined.

"Hey, Sis!" The screeching voice was followed by the pounding feet of her brother. "Finally found you. Hi, Mr. Billings. Hey, Bones looks pretty awesome. How'd you get those ribbons in his hair?" Without waiting for an answer, Jimmy rushed on. "Mom and Dad are trying to find a place to sit. I told them I'd look for you. I didn't think there'd be so many *people*." His eyes were wide.

Penny laughed and wondered how her brother could talk so fast.

"Bones'll win, though."

"You and I think alike," agreed Mr. Billings. "You've got to cheer your sister on."

"Oh, I *will*! Some pretty nice horses out there." Jimmy looked around. " 'Course, not as nice as Bones. I brought you something, Penny." He started digging in his pocket. "For good luck!" He dropped it in her hand.

Penny looked down. "What *is* it?"

"The first fly I tied. I cut the hook out, of course. But when I bring it with me fishing, I always catch a *lot*!"

Penny stared at the tiny jumble of string and feathers, then smiled at her brother. "Thanks, Jimmy. I'm sure it'll help me, too." She stuck it into her jacket pocket.

"Well, I better go find Mom and Dad and tell them where you are," Jimmy said. "You in the next class?"

"The one after."

"Okay." He started off, then turned and hurried back. "Forgot to wish Bones good luck." He gave the horse a kiss on the nose. The kiss came as a total surprise to Penny. Jimmy shrugged, got red in the face, and shot off again through the crowd.

"Well," Mr. Billings chuckled, "that lucky piece ought to see you right through."

Penny was really pleased that her brother had such faith in them. She hoped she could live up to it.

Jan had finished warming up the mare and came out of the ring. "Was that your brother?" she asked.

"Yep," Penny said with a grin.

"Then your parents are here?"

"Yeah, and I better be good."

"You won't have to take a first, Missy, to impress them," Mr. Billings said. "They'll see how far you've come."

Penny prayed he was right.

104

The jumps had been raised and rearranged for the intermediate hunter classes. The announcer called out that any intermediate riders who wished to walk the course should do so now.

"Go on," Jan said. "I'll hold Bones."

Penny went up to join the other riders walking the course. She felt self-conscious, but put her worries aside as she studied the fences and paced out the distances between them. There were a couple of tough spots, but Bones could do it if his leg was all right and he wasn't distracted.

She joined Jan and Mr. Billings, and they watched the next class from the rail. The contestants were intermediate riders on stable-owned horses. There were a dozen entries in the class. Penny's eyes were glued to each rider. She looked for problem areas. Most of the riders seemed to be having trouble with the course, especially coming up the far side. There were some difficult combinations of uprights and spreads.

Bones was watching, too. His ears were pricked toward the course, and he grew restless and stomped his feet.

"I think I'm going to walk him and get him out of the sun," Penny said to the others. She was feeling restless herself. Watching the other riders had made her nervous again. She led Bones to a grassy spot behind the barn and let him graze and relax. She prepared herself mentally.

The horses she would be competing against would probably be better than those she'd just watched. The fences wouldn't be any higher, but she'd have to ride Bones to the inch. She prayed that the last five days of not practicing wouldn't take a terrible toll.

She heard the announcer calling the next class—hers. Penny wiped her clammy hands. "Okay, boy," she said to Bones. "This is it. If we don't win, that's all right—but let's *try!*"

Bones sensed her excitement and perked his ears. By the time they got to the ring, two riders had already gone off and another was in the ring. Penny mounted. Bones pranced up to Mr. Billings and Jan.

"Good luck!" they both said.

"Eight more to go," answered Penny.

"Keep him moving," Jan said. "The worst part about riding late in a class is that your horse either gets too hyper or falls asleep. But at least you can watch the first riders. I know you'll do great!"

Twelve

Penny rode Bones over to the gate and joined the other riders waiting their turn. A couple of the riders glanced at Bones with raised eyebrows. Their mounts, Penny noticed, were perfectly built, graceful, and sleek.

Penny concentrated on the riders who were jumping. She watched for problem areas and mistakes. Several of the horses didn't perform very impressively, but that might have been due to their riders' mistakes. One of Mary Lou's friends came out of the ring scowling fiercely after a poor round.

Others did exceptionally well. Two riders had clean rounds. Penny wondered how the judges would decide on a winner if several horses went clean. On style? On time? She and Bones would have to achieve both.

Penny knew the course by heart now, but riding it perfectly was another matter. Bones was becoming frustrated and skittish again. She walked him up and down near the gate.

Finally her number was called. She trotted Bones toward the gate. He stopped dead in his tracks halfway through. He looked from side to side at the spectators in panic and huffed anxiously through his nostrils. A couple of riders giggled. The people in the stands didn't look very impressed, Penny noticed with a sinking heart.

"Come on, boy," Penny whispered urgently. "Relax. I believe in you!"

Penny tightened her legs and urged him forward. He snorted nervously but stepped into the ring and trotted forward.

The announcer boomed out, "Penelope Rodgers on Bones, Number Twelve."

The roar of the loudspeaker startled Bones. He flicked his tail and did a spirited side-step. Penny urged him on with determination.

"Good boy . . . good boy," Penny whispered. "Stay with me."

She put him into a canter as they circled toward the first jump. Bones was glancing sideways at the crowd. Penny had brought the crop. She tapped him with it. He quivered, but he pulled himself together and looked ahead to the first jump, a three-foot single rail.

They sailed over the first fence, and at last Bones settled down and forgot the crowd. Penny headed him toward the next. She'd have to guide him every inch of the way. She knew the course; he didn't. Fortunately Bones was thinking about jumping now.

They progressed down the nearside wall over a brush, a gate, and into a sharp turn. Penny cut the turn as tight as she could without putting Bones at a disadvantage. They headed on a diagonal toward a three-fence combination. Squeeze, jump, squeeze, jump, squeeze, jump. Bones was kicking his heels as he came out of the last jump. How he loved gymnastics! But the next fence before the turn was a wall. Penny had calculated it was four strides away.

Bones was covering the ground too fast in his excitement. She pulled him back and collected him, then squeezed.

He soared over the wall. They turned. They faced the series of fences that had frustrated other riders—a high, narrow gate, then an oxer, then a brush and pole, then barrels, then a turn.

By now Penny had forgotten the crowd, too. She was only aware of herself and Bones, working together.

Bones put his heart into it. He launched himself over the gate, stretched for the oxer, bounced over the brush, stretched again for the barrels. He obeyed Penny's every command as they turned for the finishing run.

Penny's movements in guiding him were subtle. They couldn't be seen from the stands. She applied gentle pressure with her hands and her legs. Her shoulders were straight. Her head was up as she looked forward to the next jump.

The last three jumps were tricky because they were unevenly spaced—three strides, four strides, two strides. Penny kept Bones collected and carefully adjusted his stride. They cleared the first two fences effortlessly. Penny squeezed hard for the last, and highest, jump. Bones vaulted and cleared it with a foot to spare.

Bones was shaking his head in excitement as Penny circled him to slow him down. She heard cries and voices, but her head felt fuzzy. She wasn't sure what any of it meant. At least they'd gotten through. She knew they'd had a clean round.

She trotted Bones out of the gate as the next and last rider came in. Penny held her head straight. She was afraid to look in any direction. She was afraid to see the expressions on people's faces.

She rode over to where Jan and Mr. Billings were waiting. They were both grinning.

"You did it, Missy! You too, Bones!" Mr. Billings took Bones's bridle and helped Penny dismount. "If you two aren't enough to make an old man proud!"

"That was an incredible ride, Penny!" Jan congratulated her.

"But other riders cleared without any faults," Penny said, still worrying.

"You guys had something special. He flew!"

Penny nearly collapsed in relief. "We looked okay, then?"

"You sure did!"

Penny suddenly remembered Bones's leg. She knelt down to examine it. "Oh, no! He's bleeding, Mr. Billings—a lot!"

Mr. Billings quickly unwrapped the bandage and examined the leg. "Hmmm," he mumbled. "Yeah, it's opened up. But nothing we can't fix. I put some bandages and salve in my car in case this happened. Let me fetch them."

Bones didn't seem to be in any pain, but Penny was anxious. She crooned to the horse as she waited for Mr. Billings to return.

"What a shame," Jan said, "and after a ride like that."

"Don't worry about us," Penny told her. "Think about your class. They're calling the advanced riders to walk the course. Here, I'll hold the mare."

"Thanks." Jan quickly strode off. Penny knew how nervous her friend must be.

The mare and Bones nickered to each other. At least Bones had something to keep his mind off his leg.

"It's going to be rough," Jan said when she'd finished walking the course.

"You'll do fine," Penny reassured her.

"I'm almost glad I'm going off second. I'm too nervous to wait any longer."

Mr. Billings hurried over with fresh bandages and salve. "You just hold him quiet, Missy, and I'll tend to his leg."

They'd attracted the attention of some of the spectators. Several people watched Mr. Billings and Bones and speculated over what had happened.

"Good luck!" Penny called as Jan mounted and headed the mare toward the gate.

Jan nodded and tried to smile, then entered the ring.

Penny's attention was divided between Bones and watching Jan ride. She didn't have a clear view of the ring, but she saw Jan clear several of the jumps cleanly.

Mr. Billings was tying off the new bandage when Jan returned. Her cheeks were flushed.

"How'd you do?" Penny asked.

"I went clean. The mare was really perky, but there're seven more to go off. Some good riders." Jan turned her attention back to the ring.

"He should be just fine," Mr. Billings said as he rose. "No harm done a few days' rest won't cure."

"Thank goodness!" Penny sighed. She turned to see her parents approaching. They were both beaming and rushed over to give Penny warm hugs.

"That was something!" her father said. "You two were better than anyone in that class. I had no idea. Congratulations!"

"Oh, Penny," her mother cried, tears brimming in her eyes. "I'm sorry I doubted you. I never thought you could teach yourself to ride like that. You were wonderful!"

"Thanks, Mom." Penny was beginning to feel teary-eyed herself. "Mom, Dad, I want you to meet Mr. Billings. He owns Bones."

"A real pleasure, Mr. Billings." Her father shook the older man's hand as her brother came charging up to join them. He was jumping with excitement. "I've been sitting under the bleachers," he said breathlessly, "listening to the judges. I think you've got it, Penny."

"Oh, Jimmy, you were probably imagining things," Penny said.

"No. I heard them!"

Penny's parents and Mr. Billings were talking quietly together. "Did you hear anything about Jan's ride?" Penny asked.

"She's got it, too."

"Now you know he's making it up," Jan butted in. "He wasn't there long enough to hear. My class just finished. Oh, wait! They're calling up the next class. I've got to watch dear old Mary Lou."

"We'll get out of everyone's way." Penny's father smiled. "We'll come back after this class.

Come on, Jimmy. You're only getting underfoot."
Her parents left, dragging a reluctant Jimmy.

"I'll see you later," Penny called to them. Her
eyes were shining. Whether she won or not, her
parents were pleased and proud of her.

Mr. Billings decided to walk Bones and offered
to take Jan's mare along, too. Jan and Penny went to
watch at the rail as the rider-owned advanced class
lined up.

As the first rider went in, Penny felt someone
shake her shoulder. She looked around to see Terry
Mullins, the stable manager.

"I've found you!" he said. "Look, someone's
dropped out of this class. I want you and Bones to
jump instead."

Penny stared at him. "Oh, I don't know, Mr.
Mullins. I don't think we're ready, and he hurt his
leg last week—not seriously, but—"

"It didn't hold him up in the intermediate," the
stable manager persisted.

"The cut opened while we were jumping." The
thought of beating Miss Boots was almost irresisti-
ble, but Penny already knew her answer. She shook
her head. "I can't take that chance with Bones. He
means too much to me."

Mr. Mullins was obviously disappointed, but he
nodded. "I understand. I'd take good care of that
horse, too. He's pretty amazing."

Penny looked over to Mr. Billings and Bones.
"He sure is."

"Well, there'll be other shows," Mr. Mullins
said. " Take a good look at your future competition."
He motioned toward the ring and rushed off.

Penny was truly stunned. She turned to Jan. "I don't believe it."

Jan winked and gave her a grin. "Mary Lou's up. I think she's the competition he was talking about."

Penny squeezed in closer to the fence as Miss Boots and Dino rode in. Penny'd never seen anyone look more confident than Mary Lou.

"Has anyone gone clean yet?" Penny asked Jan.

"Not yet. Number Three was close with a couple of ticked rails."

"Too bad," Penny mumbled.

Mary Lou started off. She took the first four fences in perfect form, turned and came up the center.

"She looks good," Penny said.

Surprisingly, Jan chuckled. "That's the easy part. Wait till she comes to the last fence combination. It's a beaut. She's been sitting back and letting Dino do all the work. She won't be able to on that last combination."

Jan was right. Mary Lou came around the last turn too relaxed and too confident. Dino saw the problem ahead before his rider did. They were too close to the fence. Dino hesitated, then made a valiant leap. He stumbled on landing. Mary Lou's smile vanished. She managed to keep Dino on his feet, but it was questionable whether they'd clear the next jump. By some miracle, the horse did it. They finished with a clean round, but with no thanks to Mary Lou.

"Guess that's it," Penny groaned. "She's the first clear round."

"Wait and watch this next rider," Jan said. "I've been hearing about him all day. His name's Bruce Logan."

Penny studied the Logan boy as he put his big bay to a canter. They went through the first half beautifully. He wasn't sleeping as he came around the last turn. He had his mount prepared for the last fences. They cleared the first and the second.

"He's going to do it," Penny whispered.

But as they went over the last fence, he ticked it very slightly.

"Oh, darn!" Penny and Jan said in unison. "Bad luck."

But the Logan boy rode off to much louder applause than Mary Lou had gotten.

"There's hope yet," Jan sighed.

Mr. Billings had brought back Bones and the mare. "Thought you girls might be needing these two—" he said with a wink, "—when you go collect your ribbons."

"If we get any ribbons," Penny said worriedly.

The judges were conferring. Someone brought a stack of ribbons to the announcer's stand. In a few minutes the announcer began calling out the winners for the pony classes. As the winners of each class were announced, they rode into the ring.

Penny licked her lips nervously, The tension was almost too much to bear. She told herself it wouldn't matter if she and Bones didn't get the blue. They'd done a good job.

The pony class ribbons were awarded. The announcer then called out the names of the winners in the first intermediate class. Those riders went out.

Penny started chewing her fingernails. She held her breath as the announcer began calling out the winners in her own class. Jan reached over and squeezed her arm.

"For Rider-Owned Intermediate," the announcer's voice boomed. "In third place, Bridget Sorenson on Jangles." He waited for the round of applause. "In second place, Michael Goldman on Eagle II." Again he waited for the applause. "And first, with an excellent, faultless round . . ."

Penny dropped her eyes. She didn't want to hear about her loss. Four riders had gone clean.

". . . Penelope Rodgers on Bones!"

"You got it! You got it!" Jan grabbed Penny's hands and danced around in a circle. Mr. Billings was patting Bones's neck and chuckling to himself.

"Get up and get out in the ring," Jan said, prodding Penny. "Bones, you old baby, you did it!"

Penny mounted and rode out in a total daze to collect her ribbon. She reined Bones up to the judges' stand and waited as one of the judges came toward them with the ribbon. Only when the judge had fastened it to Bones's bridle did Penny realize that she *had* won.

"Oh, thank you!" she told the judge. "And thank you, Bones!" This time she heard the applause. She'd done it! She and Bones had done it!

"Bones, you baby, you wonderful baby!" She rubbed his ears and leaned over and hugged his neck. The spectators gave them a louder hand of applause. She noticed as they rode out of the ring that people were looking at them differently. They

116

were suddenly appreciating this old non-Thoroughbred and his rider, she thought with a grin.

Penny rode back to where her friends and family were all waiting and dismounted. Her mother hurried over. She slid an arm around Penny's shoulders and pulled her daughter close.

"Oh, Penny, I'm so proud of you. I didn't think your riding was important because I've never been interested in it. But it *was* important. And you made all this happen yourself."

"I did have a lot of help, Mom." Penny smiled at Jan and Mr. Billings.

"You've shown us something today," her father added. "We can see now how much it means to you, and we want you to be able to ride as much as you like. We'll see if we can't help out with some of the expenses."

"Oh, Mom, Dad—thank you!" Penny felt close to tears. Her throat was choked with happiness. She couldn't get any words out.

Her brother, though, had no problem finding the words. "I *told* you how good she was!"

"Yes, you *did*, Jimmy," Penny's parents agreed.

Mr. Billings came shuffling over. His blue eyes were twinkling. "Well, if I can add my two cents here . . . your parents and I had a little talk, Missy. We decided that it was okay if I gave Bones to you—provided, of course, you keep him at my place for now, and I help feed him."

Penny looked back and forth between her parents and Mr. Billings. Her eyes were wide. "Bones—mine?"

"That's what I said. He's all yours, Missy. You deserve him."

Penny threw her arms around Bones's neck. "Did you hear that, Bones?" she whispered, wiping away her tears. "You're really mine, now—all mine!"

ABOUT THE AUTHOR

JOANNA CAMPBELL was born in Norwalk, Connecticut, where she grew up loving horses and eventually owning a horse of her own. She took riding lessons for a number of years, specializing in jumping. She's written three Sweet Dreams novels and the Love Trilogy in the Caitlin series for Bantam Books, and four novels for adults. In addition to her writing, she's sung and played piano professionally and owned an antique business. Five years ago she moved to the coast of Maine, where she lives with her two teenaged children, Kimberly and Kenneth.